MURDER
at the
playgroup

A Pippa Parker Mystery

Liz Hedgecock

WHITE
RHINO
BOOKS

For Stephen,
my right-hand man

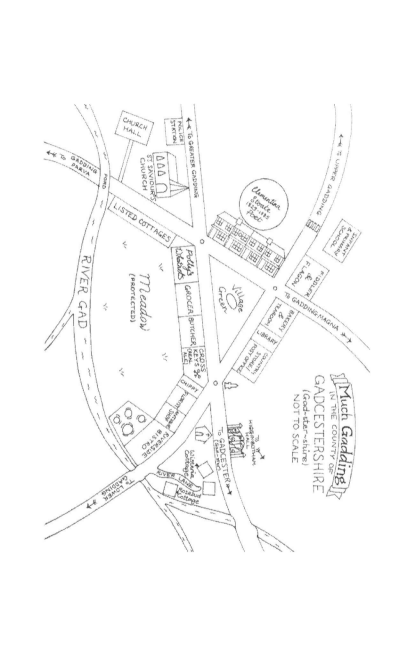

Much Gadding
IN THE COUNTY OF
GADCESTERSHIRE
(Gad-ster-shire)
NOT TO SCALE

TO GADDING PARVA
TO GREATER GADDING
TO UPPER GADDING
TO GADDING MAGNA
TO GADCESTER (Gad-ster)
To LOWER GADDING

CHURCH HALL
POLICE STATION
ST SAVIOUR'S CHURCH
SCHOOL & PRIMARY ANNEXE
Clementine Gloate
1925–1985
Poet
LISTED COTTAGES
Polly's Pantries
GROCER
BUTCHER
CROSS KEYS REAL ALE
Village Green
FIDDLER FLAGON
BAKERY
TEAROOM
LIBRARY
POST OFFICE
COUNTY STORES
Meadow (PROTECTED)
RIVER GAD
FORD
CHIPPY
FLORIST
TOY SHOP
RIVERSIDE BISTRO
Wisteria Cottage
Rosebud Cottage
RIVER LANE
THE HIGGINBOTHAM HALL
To Higginbotham Hall

CHAPTER 1

The River Gad pierces the heart of Gadcestershire. It flows wide and strong in the county town of Gadcester, deep enough for ferries, pleasure boats and pedalos to ply a tourist trade at the heritage quay. But above Gadcester, the river's tributaries are slow and narrow.

The slowest of these runs through the village of Much Gadding. It is shallow, clear, and much prized by the locals for the picturesque quality it lends to the village centre. It also lends a distinct dampness to the listed cottages in its vicinity. This is in addition to the natural climate of Much Gadding, which is inclined to rain.

A rambler on the river path would have noted an unusual addition to the scene one Friday lunchtime. That is, if a rambler were present, because it was raining the sort of fine rain that soaks you through after fifteen minutes. The river was grey, to match the sky. The vegetation was lush and green, dripping onto the path and onto the glistening, treacherous cobbles of River Lane. And backing slowly up River Lane was a bright red removal lorry, whose driver leaned out of the window, frowning, and swearing under his breath as the rain found his bald spot.

1

'It's no good, Mrs Parker,' he shouted. 'Road's too narrow to get her any further.' The lorry sighed in confirmation as he put the handbrake on, and settled to wait, rumbling to itself.

Mrs Parker rumbled too. She was standing outside a small, quaint cottage, holding a thumb-sucking toddler. An observer would have found her hard to describe, as she was wearing an overcoat which flapped round her wellies, and had a sun hat jammed low on her head. Only medium height and bobbed brown hair were visible. Oh, and expecting a baby quite soon.

'Are you sure?' She walked forward to inspect the van, and concluded, reluctantly, that if the lorry backed any further a lamp-post would be in danger.

'Sorry love,' yelled Kevin from the passenger seat. His dad dug him in the ribs. 'We'll have to carry it all up, I s'pose.'

'I'll get the kettle on.' At least she had remembered to bring the essentials box in the car. Kettle, tea, coffee, milk, mugs, chocolate biscuits and a selection of toys and snacks for Freddie, who so far had ignored them in favour of running round the house trailing his hand along the wall.

She thought of Simon, who of course was working away this week. He'd be moving round a hotel buffet right now, his hand hovering between the mini quiches and the chicken satay. 'I'm sorry, Pippa,' he'd said, running a hand through his hair and looking helpless, which is quite hard to pull off in a suit. 'Declan asked me to lead on the Biztec account. It could be big money.' Pippa's mental image of Simon filling his plate and his face was washed away by a plop, as a large raindrop flattened itself on the worktop in front of her. She put a mug on top of it, and wiped the

2

misted window. The removal men were progressing, her sofa between them. But they slowed as they reached the front door. Then they put the sofa down and their heads together.

'What is it?' called Pippa, a chill striking her heart.

'It won't go. Doorway's too narrow.'

'Can you turn it?'

The senior removal man, George, scratched his head. 'Nah,' he said eventually. 'Won't go either way.'

They stood looking at the sofa, impassive as a basking seal in brown leather.

'Could you get it back in the van for now?' said Pippa. 'I suppose I'll have to put it in storage.' *And how much else,* she thought.

'Well, we'll bring in what we can, love,' said Kevin, and this time his dad didn't nudge him. 'Cuppa tea would be lovely.'

Pippa gritted her teeth and went into the house. 'How about a nap, Freddie? The travel cot's right here.'

'No!' yelled Freddie, wriggling and thrashing his legs. 'Dooooowwwwwwwn!'

'All right.' Pippa plonked him in the cot and fetched Peepee Rabbit, Honk Honk Pig, and an assortment of noisy rattly things. Freddie grabbed a tambourine, leaned over the edge of the cot, and had a good bash at the sturdy oak door frame. Pippa pinched the bridge of her nose, then hung her coat on the banister and went through to the kitchen. Simon would probably whack his head on that beam. She didn't feel sorry at all.

It was Simon's fault they were here, anyway. Pippa had been perfectly happy in their garden flat in the London suburbs. After Freddie had come along, two-and-a-half years ago, she had reduced her hours at Positive PR to three days a week, and taken as a whole, life was good.

'I've been thinking,' said Simon, one evening, as he came in from the kitchen with a glass of wine.

'Oh?' said Pippa.

'Mm.' He sat on the sofa and Pippa rearranged her legs on his lap. 'Is London the best place to raise a family?'

'We have a park nearby, the nursery's great, and the commute isn't too bad. If there aren't leaves on the line.' Simon drank the wine, and Pippa remembered the cold, sharp taste of it.

'Yes, but — is that enough?' Simon frowned.

'What, all of London?'

'What about countryside? Wide open spaces, green fields, a slower pace of life? When I was a kid in Much Gadding . . .' Pippa leaned back, closed her eyes, and tuned out Simon's rambles over hill and dale with his mates, having adventures all day and only returning for tea.

'Maybe. We'll see,' she said, in response to his hopeful look. After all, Sunday evening wasn't really the time to be discussing life-changing plans.

Pippa threw teabags into mugs, flicked the kettle on, and pondered the series of events which had brought her, Pippa Parker, wife, mother, and former PR person, to a leaky cottage in the middle of nowhere. How could she have known that Azimuth, Simon's London-based firm, would decide to relocate to the Home Counties? 'Fifteen miles from Much Gadding!' crowed Simon. 'I mean, what are the chances?'

'What about my job?' said Pippa.

'Think of the house we could buy with what we'd get for the flat,' said Simon, his eyes fixed on an imaginary property which Pippa strongly suspected of having a white picket fence and roses round the door. 'And you'd have babysitting on tap with Mum nearby. How handy is that? Especially with number two on the way.' He rubbed Pippa's still-flattish stomach gently.

Ping! Pippa filled the mugs, noting that the water was perhaps a little speckly for most people's tastes, and squished the teabags with a spoon. While the tea brewed she went to check on Freddie, who was sitting in a corner of the travel cot, falling asleep over a book. 'Would you like a blanket, Freddie?'

Freddie opened his eyes wide. 'NOT sleepy,' he said, and blinked.

Pippa huffed as she peeled the plastic film from the top of the milk.

Curse Laurel Villa, the detached, roomy house on a very desirable road in Much Gadding (according to Sheila, her mother-in-law and the presumed provider of babysitting on tap), which had come up for sale.

Curse the efficient estate agent who had managed to sell their flat days after it went on the market. 'Such light! Such space!' he had raved when he came to do the photos, backheeling Freddie's rattle under the sofa.

Curse the buyers with no chain who had wanted to move into their flat within two weeks.

And most of all, curse this damp, poky, run-down cottage which was all the estate agent in nearby Upper Gadding had to let at such short notice.

She took the mugs of tea to the front door. Kevin and his dad were carrying pieces of wood up the winding path. 'This your bed, love?' said George.

'It was,' said Pippa.

5

'Right you are, we'll take them upstairs.' George took a mug, drank it in one go, and handed it back, making a face as he did so. 'Phoo! Two sugars next time, if you would.' The men thumped indoors, wood clattering against the banister, knocking Pippa's coat onto the floor. From behind her came the wail of a rudely awakened Freddie.

Pippa shrugged her coat on, scooped up Freddie, and found her car keys. She sighed with pleasure at Freddie's tricycle lying in the boot, its handle waiting to be attached. 'We're going for a little walk to the village,' she shouted, as Freddie wriggled free and tugged at the trike. 'We may be some time.'

CHAPTER 2

Pippa inched the trike past the removal lorry and Freddie shouted 'Aa-AA-aa-AA-ah' as he bumped along the cobbles of River Lane.

'Look Freddie, swans!' Pippa pointed to the two white swans sailing past on the river, followed at a discreet distance by two grey fluffy teenage birds, almost as big as their parents. All four ignored them completely.

Pippa had visited Much Gadding a few times, usually for summer days on the village green, or during the annual festival at Higginbotham Hall. On most of those occasions she had been too busy placating Freddie or, indeed, Sheila, to pay much attention to her surroundings. This was the first time she had explored the village as a resident. She considered a walk-by viewing of Laurel Villa, but decided the contrast between it and her current residence would be too painful.

Ahead of her was a small parade of shops, starting with the Riverside Bistro, decorated in the green, white and red of the Italian flag, and currently closed. Pippa glimpsed red and white gingham tablecloths and Chianti flasks with red candles in. Perhaps Simon was planning to take her for a slap-up meal there when he finally made it home.

Next to the bistro was an antique shop, also closed, with a spinning wheel in the window. Pippa blinked, and looked at Freddie's trike. No, it wasn't a penny farthing. She hadn't gone back in time. The next shop along was a florist (closed), followed by a fish and chip shop (closed but opening at five). On the other side of the road was a chapel, with a hut next to it.

Ahead was the war memorial, a white stone obelisk with a few tattered poppy wreaths at its foot, and beyond, the triangular village green. This, she remembered, was the middle of Much Gadding. The heart, as Sheila liked to put it. Currently, however, it was deserted apart from a few ducks swimming in circles round the pond. 'I know how you feel,' said Pippa, and suddenly a pair of ducks began flapping and quacking furiously at each other. A raindrop splashed Pippa's nose and she scanned the scene for something, anything to do. On another corner of the green was a pub with lights on, and she steered Freddie towards it.

The woman behind the bar watched Pippa and Freddie negotiate the carpeted steps. 'Afternoon,' she said. 'You've picked the wrong day for a sightseeing tour. Everything's shut on a Monday.'

'No, I, er, I — I live here.' Pippa's cheeks grew warm. 'I just moved in.'

'Oh.' Two old men in the corner stopped talking and eyed Pippa.

'Do you do coffee?'

'We do.' The woman reached round and put a menu in front of Pippa. 'Cappuccino, latte, Americano, espresso, hot chocolate, what'll it be?'

'Oh, er . . . cappuccino. Please. And a glass of milk.'

The woman ran her eyes over Pippa as if her choice was no more than she had expected. 'I'll bring it over.'

Pippa found a seat away from the big screen and the two men, and looked at Freddie. He was staring at the TV screen, and a bubble of snot expanded and contracted with every breath. He was still lovely, and she was sure they would be happy. Perhaps she had just picked the wrong day to explore.

'Here you go.' The woman set down a beaker of milk, and a cappuccino with a little biscuit on the side. 'So where are you living?'

'We're renting a cottage on River Lane until the house we're moving to is ready.'

'River Lane, eh?' The woman grinned. 'Watch out for the rats, they come up from the river. My auntie lived there and she was always going after 'em with a broom handle. You'd best get some traps. When the country store's open, of course.' Her eyes narrowed. 'You're not local.'

'No,' admitted Pippa. 'My husband grew up here, though.'

'Did he, now. What's his name? I'm from Gadding Parva myself, but I might know him.'

'Simon Parker. Do you remember him?'

The woman's eyes snapped wide open, and she grinned like the Cheshire Cat presented with a bowl of cream. 'I'll say I do! Simon Parker . . . he was in the year above me at GadMag. The high school,' she said, in response to Pippa's raised eyebrows. 'So he settled down after all . . . well, well, well.' She was still grinning. 'I'll let you drink your drink in peace.' A low, dirty laugh escaped from her as she returned to the bar, and Pippa suspected she was meant to

9

hear.

Oh God, I hadn't expected skeletons. Pippa sipped her coffee carefully, trying to avoid a frothy moustache. She glanced towards the bar. The woman was leaning against the wine fridge, texting. She looked at Pippa, then at her phone, with a little smirk on her face.

Pippa wriggled in her — Simon's — overcoat and maternity jeans. She was in the middle of moving house, what was she supposed to look like? Next time — and she had a vision of herself spending the morning at a beauty salon to get pub-ready. Simon-ready. Was this what life in Much Gadding would be like? Beating off rats, damp, and Simon's many female admirers? Pippa drank the rest of her coffee with her eyes fixed on the table, put a five-pound note under Freddie's empty beaker, and left before she could kill the woman behind the bar with her death-ray stare.

'Bye, love,' called the woman, still texting.

'Let's explore the rest of the village, Freddie.' Pippa wiped his nose, to present them in a marginally better light to any other predatory villagers. They set off again, rumbling past a row of chocolate-box cottages. One had a blue plaque: *Clementina Stoate, 1829-1885, poet, lived here*. Pippa had never heard of her.

Across the village green were more closed shops: a butcher, a greengrocer, and a shop called Polly's Whatnots, in curly rainbow script. Pippa crossed the road for a closer look, and was disappointed to discover balls of wool and paintboxes in the window. A witchcraft emporium might be more use. On the corner opposite stood a picturesque church with a spire and a large stained glass window: *St Saviour's*, proclaimed in gold on a maroon background.

Postcard cute. Indeed, a sign saying *Much Gadding Conservation Area* was the only blot on the landscape. Pippa approached the 'Parish Notices' boards, papered with leaves of all colours, some soaked through, some waving gently in the breeze.

Aerobics, she read. *Zumba. Salsa. SlimFit. Yoga.* All at St Saviour's Church Hall. This was obviously where the in-crowd went. *Gadabout Bus Service. Gadding Ramblers Club. Much Gadding Camera Club (incorporating Gadding Parva and Lower Gadding). Gadding Goslings Playgroup —*

Pippa lifted the sheet which had been pinned half over the top —

Gadding Goslings Playgroup, Tuesdays and Thursdays, 10.00-12.00. Children from 0-5 welcome. The notice had a border of very yellow geese, and a name, Barbara, with a phone number next to it.

'There we are, Freddie,' Pippa said to the top of Freddie's head. 'A playgroup for you to make new friends!' *Me too*, she thought. Friends in the same boat, who could show her the ropes. Mums who'd be too knackered to go after Simon.

The church hall was a short way down the road, next to a small ford. Pippa spied a large, square modern building set behind a row of trees. The lights were on but the door was closed, and Pippa speculated on what might be going on within. Flower arranging? Watercolour painting? Perhaps a spot of parkour, she sniggered, then checked herself. *You're the one who wants things to do.*

As if Freddie had heard, an almighty fart came from his trousers, followed by a smell which indicated that not only air had escaped. He grinned, hugely.

11

'Come on, stinkbomb.' Pippa grasped the trike's handle and did a three point turn on the concrete path.

Back at Rosebud Cottage, River Lane, George and Kevin had deposited piles of boxes in every room, on every flat surface. 'It's all in, now,' said George. 'Good job there wasn't more.'

'Mm,' said Pippa. The cottage looked even smaller now.

'We'll take your sofa to the storage unit,' said Kevin. 'The two armchairs made it in, anyway.' They stood in front of the bare fireplace, a cardboard box occupying each. He walked down the path, whistling.

George put a hand on her shoulder, then retreated as the smell from Freddie's nether regions reached him. 'We'll be off,' he said hastily. 'Give you time to settle in.'

Pippa surveyed the havoc. There was barely room to move among the boxes. She read the side of the nearest one: Sheets, pillowcases, duvet covers. The bed was in pieces and she had no idea where the duvet was. And she couldn't sleep on the sofa because it had gone.

Outside, the removal van roared into life, and Freddie, startled, let out an outraged scream.

CHAPTER 3

'Hello Pippa,' Simon's voice was warm and slightly shouty, and some sort of jazz played in the background. 'How did it go?'

'As well as can be expected.' Pippa shifted the phone to her other ear and shifted from one buttock to the other. The windowsill was cold through her jeans. 'They couldn't get the sofa in.'

'Oh well, never mind. It isn't for long.' A pause, featuring a saxophone solo. 'You're very crackly.'

'So are you. The signal isn't good, I can only get above one bar in the bathroom.' The saxophone wailed. 'You seem to be having fun.'

'Not really.' Simon lowered his voice. 'We've been workshopping since 9.30. I thought they'd want a break from us but they've taken us for drinks. Oh thank you!' A discreet slurp. 'How's Freddie?'

'He's fine, went down at half-seven. We had a chippy tea, he liked that.'

'What, doesn't the oven work?'

'No . . . I mean I didn't particularly want to cook, after packing and unpacking all day. Anyway, it's a range. I have no idea how to work it.'

'There'll be a manual,' Simon said. 'It can't be that hard. Mum could show you. Why don't you ask her round?'

'Yeah.' Pippa inspected the toes of her slippers. 'I met someone today who knows you.'

'Did you?' Simon sounded politely interested. 'Who?'

'I don't know her name but she works at the pub. Might be an old flame of yours.' Pippa kept her voice light, but she felt accusation creeping in.

Simon laughed. 'It's possible.' Someone called his name. 'I'd better go. I'm glad you're OK. Speak soon, yeah?'

'Yeah. When are you —'

'Love you!' And the phone went dead.

Pippa ate a cold, vinegary chip from the polystyrene carton balanced next to her, and scrolled through the numbers in her phone.

'Hello Pip! Are you in? What's it like in the coontryziiide?'

'Honestly? It's bloody awful so far. What are you doing in anyway, Suze?'

'It's Monday,' said Suze, disgustedly. 'Even I can't find anywhere to go on a Monday.' Suze was Pippa's best friend. She'd been a former colleague, too, till she got poached by another agency.

'Try living here. Seriously, everything except the village hall and the pub was shut.'

'Noooooo.' Pippa heard the grin in Suze's voice. 'You're having me on.'

'I wish. And guess what?'

'What?'

'Well . . .'

'Come on, what? The cottage is haunted? You've got to wash your clothes in a stream?'

'River,' Pippa corrected, automatically. 'No, it's worse than that.'

'Get away. What?'

'The woman who works at the pub remembered Simon from school. Apparently he was, well . . . I reckon she still fancies him. And she said something about him settling down.'

'And?'

'That was more or less it.' Pippa ate another chip.

'Pip, you're talking, what, fifteen years ago? She probably had a schoolgirl crush on him, that's all.'

'Mm. I wonder if she's the only one.'

'Well, what are you going to do? Make him wear a big "I'm taken" sign?'

Pippa giggled. 'It's a thought. It's just —'

'What?' Suze was frowning, Pippa could tell. 'She hasn't got you rattled, has she?'

'It's just that he's away so much, with his job and all.' *There, I said it.*

'Don't be daft. What you need is a support network. I'd come up, but I've got that mini-break in Barcelona this weekend.' Pippa felt a fierce pang of nostalgia for Gaudi, rioja and flamenco. 'Isn't there somewhere you can go to meet people? Normal people?'

'There's a playgroup . . .'

'I suppose it'll have to do. What do you do at a playgroup, anyway? Apart from play?'

'Drink tea and chat, mostly.'

'Sounds like a riot . . . Are you sure you're all right?'

15

'Yeah.' Suze was right. One barmaid did not make an adulterer. 'I'll feel better when I've got the house sorted.'

'Course you will. I wish I was closer.'

'Me too.' Pippa yawned. 'Sorry. Busy day.'

'Go on you, get your beauty sleep. I'm off to Netflix and chill.'

'Whatever. Bye, Suze.'

'Bye, Pip.'

Pippa clicked *End Call* and pulled her cardigan more closely round her bump. Of course Suze was right. She put a hand to the chilly glass, and peered out. The outline of the rooftops was visible against the indigo sky. Perhaps the neighbours would be nice, and sociable.

Tomorrow is another day, she tried to convince herself. She stretched carefully. Tomorrow she would take Freddie to the playgroup and meet nice new people. What to wear? Not jeans . . . She inspected the grubby knees of the pair she was wearing. Then again, her wardrobe was limited to maternity pants and baggy tops. Pippa mentally flicked through them and got no further than a floaty top. With earrings, and mascara.

She tiptoed across the landing to the bedroom. For now, the travel cot was set up in the corner, and Freddie lay sleeping, thumb in mouth, duvet in a tangle. George and Kevin had put the mattress on the floor, and Pippa had eventually found the duvet in a bin bag.

She eased her jeans off and lowered herself gradually onto the mattress. *I'll need a hoist soon.* In her mind the texting woman leaned forward, grinned at her, and pulled out her phone.

Simon had probably had a good few drinks now.

But he wouldn't . . .

16

Pippa rolled over and struggled to her feet, hanging on to the bedside table. Something that smelt of him, that's what she needed. She grabbed her phone and shone the torch around. A box labelled *Clothes — S* stood by the window. Pippa opened it quietly and shone a light inside. T-shirts, neatly folded. Pippa shook one out, but it smelt of nothing but fresh washing. She buried her head into the box and inhaled. Not a thing. She threw the T-shirt on top of the box, and lowered herself to the mattress.

Wrapping herself in the duvet, Pippa willed herself to sleep, which didn't work at all, and occupied herself with listening to the weird countryside noises until she was too tired for them to worry her any more.

CHAPTER 4

A shrill cry echoed in the mist. Pippa froze, one hand on the door, one grasping Freddie's mitten.

'Hello? Is someone there?'

Silence. Then a peevish, quavery voice cried 'Beyoncé tripped me!'

'Can I help?' Pippa called in the general direction the voice had come from.

'You can help me up, yes.'

Pippa edged along the path. 'Can you keep talking? I can't see you.'

An exasperated sigh. 'I'm on the doorstep of Wisteria Cottage. In a crumpled heap.' The cobbles were slippery under Pippa's feet, and she kept tight hold of Freddie. 'Are you the new person at Rosebud?'

'The new family, yes.'

'A family?' A chesty chuckle followed. 'You must be like sardines.'

Pippa peered into the mist. A dark lump hunkered in front of one of the cottage doors. 'I'm coming.'

'So's Christmas. Bloody cat.'

'Beyoncé's a cat?'

18

'Yes, and a useless mouseless excuse for a moggy she is too. My grand-daughter named her. It was that or Kardashian, and I'm not shouting that in front of the neighbours.' An arm shot out and Pippa recoiled. 'Heave-ho.'

'Stay there, Freddie.' Pippa parked him by the porch, took hold of the waving hand with both of hers, and pulled. It seemed to be making no impression until the lump suddenly reassembled itself into a spindly collection of limbs, and popped upright like a cork from a bottle.

The woman, who towered over Pippa, smoothed herself down and straightened her skirt. 'Thank you, dear.' She extended her hand. It was like shaking hands with a tree root. 'I'm Mrs Margison. You can call me Marge, if you like.'

'Er, thank you. I'm Pippa. Pippa Parker. And this is Freddie.'

Marge offered a hand to Freddie, who stared at it with eyes like saucers. 'I don't bite, young man! Well, maybe sometimes,' she cackled. 'I don't know how you'll get on in that poky cottage. I've been in a few times, and I could barely swing Beyoncé.' She glared at a slim tabby cat, sitting in front of a large bush.

'It's only till the house we're buying is available. And my husband Simon works away a lot, so mostly it'll be just me and Freddie.' Pippa wasn't sure why she had felt the need to stress she was married.

'Ohhh.' Marge inclined her head in an owlish nod. 'Wait a minute. You said Simon? Simon Parker?'

'Er . . . yes.'

'Ha! I remember him!'

Oh no.

'Yes!' crowed Marge. 'I caught him up my apple tree on several occasions! Oh he was a demon scrumper, your husband. I used to throw sticks at him, but he'd climb higher. Like that ruddy cat.' Beyoncé, oblivious, was washing her face.

'Oh. I'm sorry.' Pippa was glad of the mist as her face was burning. 'I'll make sure he doesn't do it again.'

'And what does he do now?'

Pippa tried to think of a way to explain Simon's job, which was tricky as she didn't understand it herself. 'He, um, he works for a firm called Azimuth. He's an account manager.'

'Ah. One of those sorts of jobs. Well, I must be getting on.' Marge climbed the step. 'Thank you for rescuing me, dear. Oh, and tell your husband I'll be watching out for him.' Her cackle followed them all the way down River Lane.

'Come on Freddie, we'll be late for playgroup.' The mist thinned as they approached the village green, but no-one was about. *It's a ghost village. Maybe Marge is the resident witch.* She snorted.

'My legs hurt,' whined Freddie.

Pippa sighed and picked him up.

The lights of the church hall shone through the gloom. Pippa imagined lots of toys for Freddie, and a cup of tea and a chocolate biscuit for her, and laughing and chatting with other harassed mums. She paused to savour it, and turned the handle of the plain grey door.

The sudden bright light made her blink. When she focused again a roomful of people were staring at her; mums, a couple of dads, and several toddlers.

'Er, hello?' Pippa stepped forward. 'Is this the

playgroup?'

A door at the back of the hall opened and a tall, grey-haired woman in a cashmere jumper and tweed skirt glided towards her. She checked her watch ostentatiously. 'Welcome to Gadding Goslings,' she said, in a most unwelcome voice. 'Do take a seat.'

Pippa put Freddie on the floor and sat on the nearest chair, and as the chatter restarted, she wondered what she had got herself into.

Freddie toddled towards a heap of toys and began to rummage. Building blocks, a blackboard, segments of wooden train track. Pippa checked her watch surreptitiously: three minutes past ten. So she wasn't late. Not properly late, anyway.

'Hello,' she said to the cowed-looking woman sitting in the next seat. 'I'm Pippa.'

'Hello,' The woman seemed to be trying to smile but the corners of her mouth wouldn't lift more than a few millimetres. Her eyes shifted to the small girl playing with a doll nearby. 'I'm Sam.'

Freddie plunged deeper into the toy mound, discarding a wooden rattle, an abacus, and a lone maraca before grabbing a wooden car. 'Broom!' he shouted.

'That's right, broom.' The frightening woman had materialised from nowhere. 'And who do we have here?'

Pippa choked back the swearword which had been on the point of emerging. 'I'm Pippa, and this is Freddie. Say hello, Freddie.'

'Hello Freddie!' he yelled, speed-crawling along the floor. 'Broom!'

'Mm.' The woman watched him go. 'Still in nappies, I see. And are we new to the village?'

'Yes,' said Pippa. She decided not to mention Simon, in case he had torched this woman's house or seduced her daughter.

'Indeed.' The woman folded her cashmere arms and looked down her beaky nose at Pippa. 'I must apologise, I haven't introduced myself. I'm Barbara Hamilton, and I oversee Gadding Goslings. Among other things.' She flashed a condescending little smile. 'The group runs on Tuesday and Thursday mornings, and we start at ten sharp. Except, of course, for the parents who are on the setting-up rota. You'll find the rota sheets on the board by the kitchen. Group members are expected to contribute at least every other week. That makes the playgroup run smoothly. Subs are two pounds per child, which covers tea, milk or water, toast and biscuits. The toilets and changing station are through that door,' — she pointed with the poise of a cabin crew member — 'and drinks and snacks are served at eleven. Any questions?'

Pippa put on what she hoped was a thoughtful expression. 'I can't think of anything right now, thank you.'

'Jolly good.' Barbara Hamilton nodded, in a way that expected an answering salute, and marched off to speak to a mother whose child appeared to be on the verge of tears.

Pippa looked for Freddie among the knot of children. He was on the far side of the room, setting his car on the ramp of a wooden garage. He giggled as it whizzed round and shot out at the bottom, then picked it up and sent it down the ramp again.

She strolled to the noticeboard. *Gadding Goslings*, it said at the top, in curly computer-generated script on lemon-yellow paper. There was a Setting-Up Rota, a

22

Putting-Away Rota, a Serving Rota, a Baking Rota, and a Crafting Rota (Every Other Thursday). Most of the boxes were filled with names in scrawled blue biro. What happened to parents who didn't contribute Every Other Week? She visualised some sort of group humiliation ritual, like the bit in *Mary Poppins* when Mr Banks is sacked and they punch through his bowler hat . . .

A bang made Pippa whip round. Standing in the doorway was a curly-haired woman balancing a small girl on one hip. She wore jeans, trainers, and a Metallica T-shirt. 'Sorry I'm a bit late, Barb,' she shouted in the direction of the kitchen, 'Nappy explosion. You know how it is.' She strode into the middle of the room and plonked her child, also wearing jeans and a black T-shirt, next to a round-eyed moppet in a pink dress. 'Chocolate pudding does terrible things to a child's guts,' she remarked, generally, took her phone from her jeans pocket, and sat down.

Pippa's feet carried her towards the newcomer. 'Mind if I sit here?' she asked, indicating the empty seat next to her.

'It's a free country,' the woman said, without looking up. Pippa resolved to find another playgroup, any other playgroup, even if it were on the other side of the county. The woman stopped typing, grimaced at her phone, and put it away. 'Sorry about that,' she said. 'Work email. On my day off, too,' and smiled. 'I'm Lila. I don't think we've met.'

'We just moved into the village.'

Lila waved a hand around the room. 'Are you impressed?'

Pippa shifted in her chair. 'Well . . .'

Lila's smile broadened. 'Good. You seem like someone I

23

can talk to.' She leaned forward conspiratorially. 'Don't let Sergeant-Major Barbara grind you down.' And Pippa found herself smiling in response, for the first time that day.

CHAPTER 5

The doors to the serving hatch were flung open with a clatter. 'Snack time!' cried Barbara, as a man and a woman stepped forward. 'Form an orderly queue, please!' she declaimed, shooing them to the hatch. 'Chop chop!' She clapped her hands.

'Is she always like this?' Pippa asked in an undertone, as they joined the tide of parents collecting their children from the floor.

'Often more so.' Lila said, out of the side of her mouth. 'She's a big cheese in the village. Parish councillor, chair of the WI, queen of the flower arrangers. If there's a committee, you'll find our Barb sitting on it, and probably on half the committee members too.'

Pippa muffled a snort. 'Freddie, snack time!' Freddie was stacking blocks into a tower. He kicked them over, and ambled across.

'Get ready for the Gadding Goslings Bake Off,' said Lila. 'Some of the parents are very competitive.'

They joined the queue, and as they approached the hatch Pippa saw a Victoria sponge on a cake stand, and a plate of cupcakes which wouldn't have been out of place in a bakery. 'Oh my gosh,' she said. 'I'll steer clear of the Baking Rota.'

'I just buy stuff,' said Lila. 'I'd poison people otherwise.'

Parents were shushing their children as they approached the counter, and drew ever closer to the eagle eye of Barbara. Pippa fought a terrible urge to giggle. She stared straight ahead and jumped as the man behind the hatch winked at her. She looked away, her cheeks burning.

'Oh good, Nick's on duty.' Lila waved and the man waved back. 'I'll introduce you. He's normal too. Well, what I call normal.'

Pippa peeped round the head of the mum in front of her. Nick was tall and lean, with short brown hair and dark brown eyes. He seemed friendly. He was handsome.

'When are you due?' asked Lila.

'Five weeks,' said Pippa, automatically. 'I was early last time, though.' She squeezed Freddie's hand.

'Bag packed?'

'Oh yes.'

'Not a great time to move, then.'

'We didn't have much choice. Our flat sold a lot quicker than I thought it would, and the house we're buying is still in a chain. So we're renting for now.'

Lila screwed her face up. 'Euww. Is it nice?'

It was Pippa's turn to make a face. 'Not really. Mind you, it's hard to see for all the boxes. I slept on a mattress last night because I couldn't be bothered to put the bed together.'

Lila nudged her forward. 'Come on, there's cake to be had. Morning Nick, what do you recommend today?'

'I'd have a cupcake if I were you.' Nick pointed with a

cake slice and lowered his voice. 'The sponge is a bit . . . soggy bottom. Tastes nice, though.'

Pippa examined the cupcakes, which were piled high with buttercream swirls and covered in glitter sprinkles. Her stomach did a little somersault. 'I'll take one for Freddie, but I might stick to toast.'

'Fair enough.' Nick put a cupcake and a slice of toast on an institutional blue plate. 'Don't let Barbara see you giving the lad a cake. She's very strict about healthy food for the kids.'

'I'll keep it under my hat,' said Pippa, and tapped the side of her nose.

The woman who was serving shot her a 'you're going to be trouble' sort of look, which cheered Pippa rather, and asked 'Tea or coffee?' in a chilly voice.

'Nick, you can do flat packs and stuff.' Lila took two cupcakes from the plate. 'Pippa here needs a bed assembling, or she might be having her baby on the floor.' She passed a cupcake to Bella, who licked the icing from the top like a cat.

Nick smiled. 'Yeah, I can make a bed. Have you got all the bits?'

Pippa visualised bolts in a plastic bag, and tried to remember which box they might be in. 'Yes. Somewhere.'

'I'll swap you bed assembly for a proper brew. You doing anything after playgroup, Lila? You could lend a hand.'

'For you, Nick, I'll tear myself from the frantic social whirl.' Lila turned to Pippa. 'I assume you don't mind us invading your home?'

'Are you kidding?' Pippa laughed. 'I've only had Freddie for company since I moved in yesterday.'

27

Someone behind them coughed loudly.

'All right, moving on.' Lila announced, and led the way to the chairs. Freddie took his cake, plopped onto the floor, and ate half of it in one bite. Pippa bit into her wholemeal toast with marginally less restraint. She hadn't realised how hungry she was.

'So did you and Nick meet here?'

Lila nodded, and grinned. 'You make it sound like we're an item.'

'Oh no, I didn't mean —' Pippa's cheeks burned.

'I know.' Lila swallowed her cake. 'Yes, we got talking. At first I thought he was one of those devoted househusbands with a power wife, but he's an odd fish, like me.' She lowered her voice. 'His wife died, but he doesn't talk about it. I'm only saying so you don't drop a clanger like I did once. He was very nice. But then Nick is very nice.'

'He seems nice,' Pippa agreed, looking towards the serving hatch. She was rewarded by the sight of Nick's back stooping over the sink. His slate-blue T-shirt ended in just the right place to — Stop it, Pippa! She mentally rapped herself on the knuckles with a ruler. 'I'm afraid I can't offer you lunch . . . all the shops were closed yesterday.'

'Wasn't expecting it.' A whine across the room became a wail, and Lila's head whipped round. 'Bella?' She stood up. Bella was engaged in a tug-of-war with a boy twice her size. 'Bella, stop that.'

'What's going on?' Major Barbara had appeared from nowhere again. 'That's enough!' she snapped. Neither child took any notice. 'PUT THAT DOWN!' she thundered. The boy let go and Bella fell backwards. The crack as her head hit the floor echoed round the room like a gunshot, shortly followed by a lung-busting scream.

Lila rushed to pick Bella up. 'Nicely done, Barbara,' she growled.

'Someone has to maintain discipline, Delilah.' Barbara's eyes flashed and Pippa half expected Lila to crumple to the ground, but she remained upright, rocking Bella in her arms. Bella sucked on her fingers and held the other hand out for the toy they had been fighting over. Lila bent her knees to get it, but Barbara was already there —

'*What* is this?' She brandished a small plastic steering wheel, its lights flashing. 'Who has brought this — thing — into the playgroup?'

No-one spoke. Everyone's eyes were fixed on the steering wheel, which beeped.

'The No Plastic Toys rule is clearly displayed on the noticeboard.' Barbara's knuckles were white as she gripped the wheel. 'There is no excuse for this.'

Still no-one spoke.

'I am waiting for an answer. Who has brought this toy?'

'Come on, Barbara —' The smile left Lila's face as Barbara spun round to face her.

'Was it you?'

'No, but I don't see why it's such a big deal.'

'My playgroup, my rules. Plastic is a pollutant and this sort of attention-grabbing toy is designed to pollute children's minds.' She brandished the steering wheel. 'Someone had better own up, or I will close playgroup for the day.'

Go on, then. Pippa reached for her coat as a small voice said 'I brought it.'

'You, Imogen?' Barbara's voice was incredulous. 'But

29

you've been coming for, what, a year?'

'It's his favourite toy,' said a slight woman with fluffy blonde hair. Standing in front of her was the large small boy who had been the other half of the tug-of-war. 'He won't leave the house without it.'

'You know the rules.' Barbara held out the toy to her. 'You had better leave, and I will consider whether I am prepared to allow you back.'

Imogen snatched the toy from her hand and gave it to the little boy, who hugged it tightly, looking at her with large, scared eyes. 'Come on, Henry,' she said, soothingly. 'Let's go and find an ice-cream.'

The room was silent as they left, except for a small beep from Henry's toy, followed by a snort and a mutter of 'Typical!' from Barbara. Then everyone made a show of small talk. Pippa was relieved when Barbara clapped her hands and announced Putting-Away Time.

Her relief was short-lived. 'Ah, Pippa.' God, the woman could materialise at will. 'You haven't put your name on the rota yet. As Imogen was due to bake on Thursday, I'm sure you won't mind filling in. Cakes or biscuits, either are acceptable.' And Barbara strode off to instruct a pair of mums on the best way to stack toys in the cupboard.

'Now's your chance to bake her a poison cookie.' Pippa jumped for the second time that minute, as a low voice tickled her ear. Nick grinned at her. 'Go on, you know you want to.'

'Don't tempt me,' said Pippa, darkly.

CHAPTER 6

'I hope you don't mind a few bits in your tea,' Pippa elbowed the bedroom door open and put her tray down. 'I did strain it, but there might be a few lurkers.'

'Nearly done,' Nick said, indistinctly. He turned his head towards Pippa and she saw the cause; a long screw protruding from the corner of his mouth like a cigarette. Her stomach did a little flip.

Lila was playing snap with Freddie, Bella, and Nick's daughter Grace, a leggy child with neat blonde plaits. 'Right, this game, winner gets a biscuit. I'll deal.' She riffle-shuffled the pack of cards and dealt rapidly.

Nick slotted the screw from his mouth into the bed frame. 'Vegas rules, Lila?'

'Of course.'

'I can't believe you've done it so quickly.' Pippa regarded the bed, which appeared sturdy and had right angles in the right places. It had taken her longer to find the bag of nuts of bolts than it had for Nick to assemble it.

'Beds are easy.' Nick stepped over the bed frame and gathered the bundle of slats lying in the corner. Within seconds he was heading for the mattress. 'Do you need a

31

hand making it?'

'I can manage that, thanks.' The words came out before she had time to think. 'Sorry. I didn't mean that in a rude way.'

'S'OK.' He grinned and Pippa handed him a cup of tea. 'Wow,' he said, peering into it. 'Is that a tadpole?'

Pippa clutched her hair in despair. 'I take it your water supply isn't like that?'

Lila and Nick both shook their heads. 'I'd get your landlord round if I were you,' said Lila. 'Especially with a young kid, and in your condition.'

'I'll phone the estate agent.' Pippa sipped her tea cautiously. 'Good job we're not here for long. I'll check how the exchange is going, too.'

'So what does your husband do?' asked Lila.

Pippa was about to give the usual 'he works for X as an X' reply, but something stopped her. 'I'm not entirely sure,' she said. 'It involves staying in hotels, schmoozing clients, and talking about "closing the deal" and "getting the numbers". Oh yes, and conference calls "across the pond" in the evenings. And me picking up his dry cleaning.'

'Maybe he's an international spy,' said Lila. 'The schmoozing is a cover.'

'Maybe. Simon Parker, man of mystery . . .' said Pippa. She imagined a Bond-girl type draping herself over Simon. 'Or maybe not. Anyway, why do you keep going to the playgroup? It's like a dictatorship.'

'I know,' said Lila. 'If it was just me, you wouldn't catch me dead in there.'

'I won!' cried Grace. 'I get the biscuit!'

'Indeed you do,' said Lila, handing her a chocolate

digestive from the pack. 'Now, Grace, as the winner you get to deal the cards this time. Let's see if you three can play on your own.' Grace collected the cards and shuffled them, dropping several. 'That should hold them for a bit,' she said, quietly. 'The playgroup is the only social space for pre-school kids in the village. I mean, the nursery fees are ridiculous, and the pre-school doesn't start till they're three. Plus I imagine you can guess who's on the board of the pre-school.'

Pippa's heart sank. 'She's everywhere, isn't she?'

'She is.' Nick's mouth set in a hard straight line. 'She's a governor at the primary school too. So if you want your kid to go to the local school, you stay on the right side of Barbara.'

'But . . . aren't there policies about school allocation?' Pippa frowned. All that seemed years away.

'There are. But I remember a couple of years ago, one of the mums at the playgroup had a massive run-in with Barbara. Seriously, it was like High Noon. Her daughter was going to the local school, but a week later she got a letter saying there'd been a mistake, and Maisie actually had a place at Lower Gadding.'

Pippa shivered. 'Where's that?'

'Three miles down the road. Far enough to be a complete pain in the neck. Could be a coincidence, but everyone reckoned Barbara had had a word in high places.' Nick gulped his tea. 'I'd just moved here and, well, let's say it left an impression on me.' He looked across at the children, who were absorbed in their game. Grace's biscuit, now a crescent moon, lay abandoned on the carpet.

'Yeah,' Lila said softly. 'There are playgroups and activities in the other villages, and I make sure Bella goes

33

to some of those. But they're a funny lot round here. If you're not in the playgroup, it's like you're not one of us. Bella didn't get asked anywhere till we'd been at playgroup for a few weeks.'

'That's ridiculous.' Pippa felt herself heating up, like a simmering kettle.

'Yup. But that's how it is.' Lila untucked her legs from underneath her and reached for her phone. 'I'm going to text Imogen and invite her to mine. I bet no-one else will until she's allowed back into the inner circle. The fear of Barbara is strong.'

'Maybe I *should* poison her,' mused Pippa.

Nick spat his tea across the room, and began to cough.

'I was joking,' said Pippa. 'Although it would get me out of any more baking.'

'I already gave you my recipe,' said Lila. 'Supermarket goodies, can't beat 'em.'

'There's a supermarket? Where?'

'Near Greater Gadding,' said Lila. 'You wouldn't catch me paying village prices. My budget's got to stretch as far as it can. My ex is crap at remembering his payments.'

'I'm hungry . . .' Freddie whined.

'After a big cupcake, and biscuits?' Pippa ruffled his hair. 'Well, it is past one o'clock.'

'Let's go out for lunch,' said Nick. 'The tearoom's not too expensive and they have lots of options for kids. It's on the corner of the green,' he said, in response to Pippa's bemused look. 'We could show you and Freddie the rest of the village afterwards, if you like. It won't take long.'

'Yeah, we can give you the guided tour of Much Gadding.' Lila grinned. 'Fifteen minutes, not including the intermission.'

34

Pippa giggled. 'It's a deal!'

'Are there beans?' asked Freddie.

'The tearoom has baked beans, yes,' said Nick, solemnly. 'And they also have . . . toast.'

'Beans on toast!' shouted Freddie. 'Come on, Mummy!' He grabbed Pippa's hand and pulled her towards the stairs.

As Pippa let Freddie lead the way to the front door, she wondered why she felt so much happier. Was it because she'd found friends? She already felt so much less alone than she had the day before. When the removal van had left she had nearly burst into tears, and only the thought of Freddie's worried little face had kept her from it. One day, maybe, she would be able to cheer up a newcomer at the playgroup, and tell her where the tearoom was, and the supermarket, and give her the tour.

She got the changing bag, opened the front door and waited for the others. Bella was jumping down the stairs, with Lila following. She glimpsed Grace behind Lila. And bringing up the rear, seeming taller in the poky little stairwell, was Nick, partly in shadow, which accentuated his cheekbones and the line of his jaw — NO, Pippa! BAD Pippa! Pippa imagined the scolding she would get from Barbara, and tried to keep her face straight. 'Coat on, Freddie.' She allowed herself a little secret smile as she put his arms into the sleeves and fastened the toggles. 'And off we go!'

'It's a shame your husband isn't here!' a voice shouted. 'He'd be useful right now.' Pippa recognised the querulous tones of Marge.

'Is something the matter?' called Nick.

Marge flung an arm to the sky. 'It's that good-for-nothing cat! She won't come for her medicine. Beyoncé!' She held up a small tin of cat food and tapped a fork against it. Beyoncé peered from a high branch.

'Beyoncé!' called Grace. 'Puss-puss!'

'Bonsay!' yelled Freddie.

'Cat!' screamed Bella. 'Come here, cat!'

'Could I have the tin please?' asked Nick. Marge huffed and handed it to him. 'Step back, everyone, and be quiet,' he said, and put the tin at the foot of the tree. Beyoncé leaned forward, inspected the ground, and within a minute, following two leaps of faith and a perpendicular run down the trunk, she was wolfing her food.

'My hero!' exclaimed Lila, flinging a hand to her brow.

Marge frowned at her, shambled forward, and seized Beyoncé round her middle. 'That's enough from you,' she said, in no particular direction. Beyoncé meowed and pawed the air. 'You can have the rest indoors,' Marge told her. 'Thank you.' She inclined her head graciously towards Nick, then plodded towards Wisteria Cottage. 'Shush, Beyoncé.'

'Well, that was exciting,' said Lila. 'I'm not sure the tearoom will measure up.'

'Beans on toast!' shouted Freddie.

'Quite,' said Nick. 'Onward!'

36

CHAPTER 7

Pippa's mobile rang as she was extracting her third attempt at a lemon drizzle cake from the oven. Lemon drizzle cake was her failsafe, her I-can-do-this-with-my-eyes-closed bake. In fact, it was the one cake that consistently worked. But not on a range cooker.

It had been so long since she'd baked it that Pippa had to check the ingredients on her phone. It was a wrench to leave the tearoom, and the pleasant, easy chat with Lila and Nick, but a big shop was necessary if she didn't want scurvy.

'Do you need help with the bags?' asked Nick.

Pippa briefly considered being a damsel in distress, dismissing the idea with regret. 'I'm sure someone will help,' she said, bravely.

'It's on the main road to Greater Gadding,' said Lila. 'You can't miss it.'

And so, after a short stroll around the village and a play on the green for the children, Pippa secured Freddie's sticky hand and they set off home. Pippa's red Mini, parked outside, was already spotted with bird droppings, and now resembled a poisonous toadstool rather than the smart city runabout of her previous life. Pippa prayed for a car wash at the supermarket, loaded Freddie into his carseat, and eased herself behind the steering wheel.

It felt strange to be in the car again and heading out of the village, after venturing no more than a few yards from the cottage. Pippa turned the radio up and sang along to Rick Astley, and Freddie's feet drummed gently on the back of her seat in time with the music. Pippa found herself smiling. She'd made friends, and she had a bed to sleep in tonight, and she was going to buy food and bake, like a proper mum.

The route to the supermarket was as easy as Lila had promised. The trickiest part was finding the road to Greater Gadding. Six roads led off the village green, which acted as a large triangular roundabout. Pippa's mission wasn't helped by the signposts, which had been designed for quaintness more than legibility. However, two laps of the triangle later, they were on their way.

Pippa was surprised at how quickly the chocolate-box conservation area of Much Gadding transformed into estates of identikit modern housing. The house they were waiting to move into was an Edwardian villa, but Pippa had refused to consider anything which hadn't been modernised. 'Freddie and Bump will be enough of a project,' she said firmly, and Simon had nodded meekly, which had pleased her at the time. *I won that battle*, she had thought at the time, trying to hide her glee as she added more and more features to her property search. *You lost the war, though, didn't you,* said a malicious little imp inside her, one wakeful night. It was a phrase which she recalled more and more as the weeks went by, and still the chain dragged on.

38

The houses kept coming on both sides. Pippa rounded a corner and a bright plastic sign popped into view. 'Here we are, Freddie!' she sang. 'Let's go and shop!'

'Wee wee,' said Freddie, disconsolately.

'Never mind,' said Pippa, indicating left and slowing for the car park entrance.

'Big wee weeeee . . .' Freddie sobbed. From the rapidly spreading smell, Pippa concluded that he was correct. She accelerated a little, looking for a parent and child space, and parked close to the store.

'Come on, let's sort you out.' She unbuckled Freddie, whose trousers were damp on one side. *Please, let there be spares.* 'Freddie, come along now.'

Freddie sulked. 'Pick up.'

'Freddie, you're all wet. You can walk, and hold my hand like a big boy.'

'PICK UUUUP!'

'No!' snapped Pippa.

Freddie banged the armrests with his fists, and his face went as red as the Mini. 'PICK UP!' he screamed.

'NO!' Pippa shouted. She heard a tut, and a woman with a pram passed by. 'Just you wait,' she muttered. 'I hope your kid has a meltdown in the deli aisle.'

Cheered by this thought, she hoicked Freddie straight out of the carseat and onto his feet. He was so surprised that he stopped crying. 'There.' She grabbed a suspiciously damp hand and marched him along.

Pippa thanked the guardian angel of her changing bag, which did contain spare pants, and smiled at Freddie, who grinned and produced a little fart. 'You're not planning a poo poo, are you Freddie?'

Freddie shook his head. 'No poo poo,' he said,

39

solemnly. 'BAD poo poo.'

'Excellent. Let's find a trolley.' Pippa wondered if she was saying the words for Freddie's benefit, or to remind herself of what she should be doing.

Freddie pulled her towards a small trolley abandoned near the entrance. 'No Freddie, a big one.'

They progressed calmly through fruit and veg, dairy, and canned goods before Pippa remembered the cake. 'Self-raising flour, caster sugar, eggs, lemons . . .' she read off her phone. 'Maybe I should make two.' She switched her half-dozen eggs for a dozen. 'Hmm . . .' Should she buy something ready-made? Ahead was the bakery aisle, with all sorts of individually-sized goodies, and of course the posh counter at the end with royal-iced monsters and a rainbow of cupcakes. She could make a sodding cake. Her baby brain wasn't that bad.

Maybe just in case . . .

'Cake!' shrieked Freddie, pointing at a packet of bright green shrink-wrapped cake bars.

'Not likely,' Pippa told him. 'Barbara would have a fit.'

'Cake!' Freddie insisted.

'These ones?' Pippa showed him some cherry bakewells.

'No! CAKE!'

Pippa sighed and added both packets to the trolley, with some Battenberg slices for good measure.

And now here she was with a bin full of cake and a shrilling mobile. She banged the tin on the range top and reached for the phone. *Simon.*

'Hello?' she panted.

'In a rush, are we?' Simon laughed, his voice crackling.

'I'm baking.'

'I won't be long,' Simon said, in an injured tone. 'I thought you'd want to chat.'

'I do, but —' Pippa glanced at the cake. 'Is it important?'

'I can get home this weekend.' He made it sound like a big achievement, not a working pattern.

'Oh good.' Then alarm bells unconnected with the cake rang. 'Wait. Do you mean you might have been working?'

'Well, Bill was talking about an all-dayer on Saturday, and you know what the trains are like on Sundays, it would hardly have been worth it. But anyway, it hasn't happened.'

'I could go into labour any moment.'

'No you couldn't, you've got two months to go.'

'Five weeks, Simon. Time flies when you're having fun. Now, I've got a cake to deal with. I'll ring back.'

Please let this one be just right. The manual for the range cooker had proved elusive, and it had taken Pippa half an hour to work out how to turn it on. She and Freddie had dined like kings on charred fish finger sandwiches and baked beans (more beans, no wonder Freddie farted like a trouper), and she had allowed him an evil green cake bar for pudding. Maybe he would do a green poo at playgroup. That was probably grounds for expulsion. She imagined smuggling a suspiciously dayglo nappy from the church hall, and laughed so hard she almost cried. Only Freddie's solemn face brought her round, and she read him a whole story and did three songs at bedtime to make up for Mummy's sillies.

She had put the first cake in the top oven, and it was still raw after an hour and a half.

She had put the second cake in the bottom oven, and it

41

came out with a top dry and cratered like the surface of the moon.

She approached the third cake with caution, like an apprentice lion tamer. She had fussed over it as if she were hatching an egg, but it seemed to have paid off. The cake was golden brown. The top had a nice break along the middle, showing a seam of paler cake, and it looked moist. The syrup stood ready in a shiny saucepan.

'A few holes for the syrup to soak into,' Pippa declaimed, smiling to camera, 'and leave in the tin to cool.' She found a skewer and inserted it by the seam. It went in easily, and emerged with no mixture sticking to it.

'Yes,' breathed Pippa. Now another hole . . . nice and symmetrical . . .

The skewer was halfway into the cake when the phone shrilled. Pippa jumped and the skewer gouged a huge lump of cake onto the floor.

'Bollocks!' shouted Pippa. She reached for the phone automatically. Simon again. She jabbed at the *Refuse* button and slammed the phone onto the worktop. Tears welled up. It was so bloody unfair, and she'd tried so hard . . .

'Mummy?' A little voice floated downstairs.

'It's all right, Freddie.' Pippa wiped her eyes with the back of her hand and went upstairs. 'Mummy was making a cake and it went a bit wrong. I didn't mean to shout.' She leaned over the travel cot and stroked his cheek. 'Silly Mummy.'

It's only a cake.

'I was scared.' Freddie said, gripping his duvet, eyes wide.

Pippa, racked with guilt, smoothed his hair. 'Don't be

42

scared.'

'Can I come in your bed?'

'Yes,' she said, and resigned herself to a night of wriggling. 'Let me tidy up first.'

Perhaps half the cake was usable. She cut the gouged bit off and binned it, doused the cooling cake in syrup, and put the tin in the oven for safety. Knowing her luck, if she left it out mice would eat it, or Beyoncé would kidnap it. She picked up her mobile. She should probably say goodnight to Simon. But when she pressed *Call Back*, the phone was engaged.

CHAPTER 8

'Hi!' Lila stood on the step, holding Bella's hand, but she was a different Lila from two days ago. This Lila wore a pale blue satin shirt, wide black trousers and ballerina pumps, and her hair had been tamed. 'I thought I'd call for you and we could walk to Goslings together.'

'We're nearly ready.' Pippa wiped a trace of — *something* — from Freddie's cheek. 'Just my shoes.' She hooked one with her foot and slid it on, then peered around for the other. 'It's here somewhere.'

'Over there.' Lila pointed.

'Oh yes. Thanks.' Pippa stepped into it. 'You look nice.'

'Work day, and I've got a meeting,' said Lila. 'I'll have to go at eleven and drop Bella at my sister's on the way.'

'Oh, right.' Pippa was suddenly glad the hall lacked a mirror. She didn't want to see herself next to Lila, though she had put on the best of her maternity wear and washed her hair that morning.

And why did you do that?

She slapped down the snarky voice in her ear.

Nothing to do with anyone in particular?

'Let's go, we'll be late. Oh, the cakes!' Pippa hurried to the kitchen — as far as a very pregnant woman can hurry, she thought disgustedly — and returned with the cake, now in a proper tin, and the packets, minus the green ones. She spent a few seconds surveying the reusable bags lounging in the corner, and chose a retro fruit-print hessian one. Ugh. Why should she care what impression the bag made? But she didn't put it back.

'Did you make a cake yourself?' Lila pursed her lips in a whistle.

'I tried.' Pippa got her keys and bag, and shooed Freddie outside. 'Unfortunately Simon decided to practise long-distance cake sabotage, so half got binned.'

'What did he do?' Lila slowed her step to match Pippa's.

'Rang while I was drizzling.'

'Ah.'

Pippa walked on a few steps. 'He rang to say he can come home this weekend.'

'That's nice of him.' Normally Pippa would have resented the hint of snark in Lila's voice, but today she found herself agreeing.

It had taken Freddie a long time to get to sleep the night before. 'I miss Daddy,' he'd whispered, and Pippa didn't have to look at him to see the wide, wondering blue eyes seeking an answer.

'I know,' she'd said. 'He'll come home this weekend.'

'When?'

'He didn't say. Probably Saturday. Or maybe even Friday.'

'What day is today?'

'Wednesday. Well, late on Wednesday. It might be

45

Thursday now.'

'Is Friday after Thursday?'

'Yes.'

'Friday, then.' And Freddie had snuggled down in her arms, right in the middle of the bed. Pippa was on the brink of sleep when she realised what she hadn't said.

I miss him too.

They were five minutes early for playgroup, and the door of the church hall was open. Inside two parents were supervising a gaggle of children in the middle of the room. The rest scurried like worker ants, setting out the toys.

'The train track goes on the right hand side, Eva,' Barbara leaned through the serving hatch, hands on the sill. No doubt she would never put her elbows on it.

'I brought cake,' she said.

'Ah, good.' Barbara beckoned her over. She drew out the cake tin and the corners of her mouth turned up. They fell again as she lifted the lid. 'Didn't we deserve a whole cake?'

'Someone rang me and caused a cake-related incident,' said Pippa.

Barbara replaced the lid. 'Well, it smells very nice,' she said, inclining her head. 'Thank you for actually making something.' She glanced towards Lila, who grinned back, completely unabashed.

Freddie, Bella and Grace played nicely with the garage and a dolls' house, while the grown-ups chatted. Pippa looked for Imogen and Henry, but they were missing, as Lila had predicted. The atmosphere was less tense than it had been on Tuesday, possibly because Barbara was mostly absent.

'I wish she'd stay in the kitchen,' Pippa muttered to

Nick.

'She won't,' said Nick. 'Too busy sticking her nose into other people's business. She'll be causing a scene any minute, just you wait and see.'

The morning wore on. The children played, bumped heads, cried, had nappies changed, were taken to the toilet, and carried on playing. Apart from the occasional smells and collisions, it was almost too perfect.

'Shit!' Lila checked her phone. 'It's gone eleven. I'd better get moving.' She grabbed her bag from under the chair. 'Bella! Time to go.' Bella's face crumpled. 'No, it really is. I'll be late.' She held a hand to Bella. 'Catch you later.' And she towed Bella away.

'I thought snack break was at eleven,' Pippa said, absently.

'It is.' Nick glanced at the serving hatch. 'Maybe we do need Major Barbara to keep us in order, after all.'

'I'll go and put the cake out.' Pippa said. Sam, the woman she had sat beside on her first visit, clapped a hand to her mouth.

'It's me! I'm serving today! Oh no, she'll have a right go.' She sprang up, half-ran to the door at the back of the hall, and flung it open, revealing a short corridor. Presumably the kitchen led off it.

Pippa rose carefully, and followed at a more sedate pace. She reached for the door handle, but it swung back. Sam stood in the gap, panting. 'Are you all right? You —'

'Come and see,' whispered Sam. Her eyes were like saucers, and her face was white. She opened the kitchen door and pointed.

Barbara was lying on the floor near the sink. She was face-down, slightly twisted, with one arm flung out.

Pippa's heart missed a beat. 'Barbara!' She rushed forward and lowered herself to her knees. She peered under Barbara's arm. 'Oh my God. She isn't breathing.' She held her hand in front of Barbara's mouth and nose, but felt no air at all. She tried to find a pulse. The limp wrist she held was still quite warm.

'Maybe she's had a stroke? Or a heart attack?' Sam watched from the doorway.

'We must ring an ambulance. Is anyone here a doctor?'

'I'll check.' Sam disappeared. Pippa kept feeling for a pulse, first in Barbara's wrist and then in her neck. Nothing.

Sam stuck her head round the door. 'No doctors, or nurses. Caitlin's phoning 999.'

Pippa looked at Barbara's still form. 'I think it's too late.' She used the handles of the cupboard to pull herself up.

Sam's hands flew to her mouth, and she vanished again.

Pippa glanced at the body as she left the room. Somehow, she still expected it to move, for Barbara to stir, and wake. All the TV shows and films, and yet she'd never seen a real dead person before. Pippa felt guilty for not being upset, even though she barely knew her.

All eyes turned to Pippa as she opened the door to the main hall. 'Is she —?' asked Nick. Pippa nodded.

The children were still playing in the middle of the room. Pippa sat down next to Nick. 'What should we do?' she muttered. 'We can't let the kids see.'

'No . . .' Nick rubbed the back of his neck. 'I know. When the ambulance arrives, you and Sam go to the kitchen with them and tell them how you found her. We can clear out with the kids — I'll take Freddie if you want

48

'— and all meet at the tearoom. Or the pub. Whichever.'

'Sounds like a plan.' Suddenly, Pippa felt weary. She watched Freddie bounce a rag doll along the floor. Two of the mums nearby were talking under their breath.

'I can't believe it. Can you believe it?'

'No. I mean, she wasn't the sort of person to *die*.'

Five minutes later the long wail of an ambulance grew louder and louder, then abruptly shut off. The children gasped and pointed as a paramedic in overalls opened the door. Some of the mums exchanged glances as he stepped in, followed by a shorter, stockier man carrying a defibrillator. 'We're here about a reported collapse.'

Sam stood up. 'I found her, I'll take you to the kitchen. But Pippa thinks she's dead.'

'Pippa?' The second paramedic scanned the room.

Pippa raised a hand. 'She isn't breathing, and I can't find a pulse —'

'I thought it might be a stroke,' said Sam, looking serious.

'Well, let's go and see, shall we.' Paramedic 1 strode towards the door.

'Can we go?' asked Nick, indicating the children, who had stopped playing and were watching the paramedics, silently.

'Could you stay put for a moment, please,' said Paramedic 2. 'If you two ladies will come with me.' He opened the door and surveyed the various other doors along the corridor. 'Where is she?' he asked, in a low voice.

Sam pointed at the kitchen door and he opened it.

'All right. Have you moved her?'

'No, not at all,' said Pippa.

'Mm. You can go back to the hall now.' They slunk back down the corridor.

In the hall people were whispering, one eye on the door.

'I hope we can go soon,' Sam whispered. 'I mean, it's not as if there's anything we can do.'

Caitlin nodded and her black bob swung. 'Yes. It's sad, but . . .'

After what seemed like hours, Paramedic 2 appeared, phone in hand. 'Well, you were right,' he said to Pippa. 'We're doing our best, and we'll keep trying, but she's not responding.'

'Can we go?' asked Sam, half-rising. 'While you, er, sort things out.'

The paramedic's eyes swept the room. He had an odd, set, expression on his face. 'No,' he said at last. 'Nobody's going anywhere.'

CHAPTER 9

'Count yourselves lucky,' said PC Horsley, rocking on the balls of his feet. 'If there weren't children to consider, you'd be coming to the station with me. As it is, I need your names and contact details. ID, if you have it on you. We'll be calling you in for statements.'

Sam gasped. 'So it's —'

'Yes. It is.' He surveyed the room. 'I'll use that table in the corner.' He picked up two chairs and carried them with him. 'One by one, please. I take it this is all of you? No one left before the, er, discovery?'

'Someone did!' Caitlin cried. 'Lila went, just past eleven. She works on Thursday afternoons.'

The policeman raised an eyebrow. 'So, this Lila, she normally leaves then, does she?'

'No, she was a bit late today. She usually goes at snack break . . .' Caitlin's voice tailed off as she realised where the conversation was heading. 'Oh dear.'

The policeman sat down and pulled out a notebook and pen. 'Names and contacts please, one at a time.' He did a headcount with his pen. 'Nine . . . plus one. Lila. Can someone give me her details?'

A few raised hands. 'Good.' He pointed at Nick with his pen. 'I'll start with you, and work clockwise.'

Nick unfolded himself from the chair, and strolled over. Pippa watched, and looked away to find everyone else doing the same. Someone commented about the weather, and they made desultory small talk until Nick's footsteps regained their attention. He smiled wanly at Pippa.

PC Horsley coughed in her direction.

'Me next, then,' she said, getting to her feet. PC Horsley waited, his pen poised.

'Pippa Parker,' she said. 'Rosebud Cottage, River Lane, Much Gadding. I don't know the postcode.'

The policeman frowned. 'How come?'

'I moved in on Monday.' He raised his eyebrows. 'We're renting while the sale goes through on the house we're buying.' His eyebrows stayed raised as he made a note.

'Phone number?'

She recited her mobile number.

'Landline?'

'It isn't connected. We didn't think it was worth it.'

He made another note. 'ID?'

Pippa rummaged in her bag and pulled her driving licence from her purse. 'Different address,' commented PC Horsley, making a note. 'You need to sort that out, Pippa Parker.'

'I will, when I've got a permanent address,' Pippa countered.

The policeman regarded her from under his eyebrows. 'Yes.'

Pippa leaned forward. 'Are you sure it's a murder?'

PC Horsley nodded. 'Depressed cranial fracture, from a

52

blow to the back of the head. Not really accidental, is it.' He put down his pen. 'The doc will do a proper exam, but the paramedics reckon she was knocked out cold. I suppose that's something.'

'Yes,' said Pippa.

'And you were one of the people who found her, I understand?'

Suddenly Pippa found it hard to swallow. 'Sam and I went to serve the snacks. Sam opened the door, and called me at once.'

'Was that the first time you visited the kitchen?'

'Yes.'

'Did you see anyone else go to the kitchen?'

'No.' She squirmed in her chair. 'I don't know. The toilets are along the same corridor. Someone might have, I wasn't paying attention.'

He stopped writing, and sighed. 'Send the next one up.'

Half an hour later, after a short lecture from PC Horsley about staying close at hand and keeping their phones switched on, the group were standing outside the church hall. Everyone looked bewildered. 'Pub?' said Nick.

'Yes,' said Caitlin. 'We wouldn't all fit in the tearoom, anyway. So we don't have to feel bad.'

'Which pub?' asked Sam.

'The Fiddler,' said Caitlin. 'The Cross Keys is an old man's pub.'

The Fiddler — the Fiddler and Flagon to be exact — was the pub Pippa had gone to on her first day in Much Gadding. Her heart sank a little as they entered, but instead of the texting woman, a lanky lad bobbed behind the bar. He whistled as they trooped in. 'I'll put some tables together for you,' he said, raising the bar flap. 'Are you stopping for lunch?' A quick conference of whispers and nods. 'I'll get you some menus. Raise hands if you need a high chair.'

A few minutes later they were settled at a collection of rickety tables, and drinks were on the way. Pippa scanned the laminated menu. 'What would you like, Freddie? Sausage, beans and chips?'

'Yeah!' beamed Freddie. Not beans again! But beans were the only veg on offer. 'Would you like peas instead, Freddie?'

'No! Beans!' Freddie banged the tray of his high chair.

'Beans it is.' Pippa flipped the menu over. 'Lasagne for me. God, I'd love a glass of red wine to go with it.'

'Surely you could have one,' said Sam.

'Probably,' said Pippa. 'But I worry about driving. In case I go into labour and have to get myself to hospital.'

'I s'pose.' The barman came with a tray of drinks and set a glass of red in front of Sam. 'Sorry.'

'S'all right,' said Pippa, as her glass of still mineral water arrived. 'Should be used to it by now.'

'Mummy's got a baby in her tummy!' shouted Freddie, pointing.

'Yes, I have. And please don't shout, Freddie.'

'Here's some crayons, and activity sheets,' said the barman, plonking down plastic pots filled with odds and ends of colour. Within seconds the children were upending the pots and snatching at crayons.

'What did you think of the policeman?' Pippa asked, generally.

'Bit full of himself,' said Caitlin. 'He's new. Norman retired . . . last year? Anyway, Norm was dead friendly, always said hello. He helped at all the community events. I

54

reckon this one's trying to be Hercule Poirot or something.' She shivered. 'It's creepy, isn't it.'

'I was trying not to think about it,' said Sam. 'Are they sure it was —' She mouthed 'murder'.

Pippa nodded. 'I asked. Apparently' — she leaned in and lowered her voice — 'Barbara was whacked on the head.'

'No!' Sam exclaimed, her mouth an O. 'That means —'

'What?' asked Caitlin.

'Don't you see?' Sam looked round the group. 'The fire exit is in the corner of the main hall. The only other door is the front one, and none of the windows open more than a couple of inches.'

Pippa swallowed. Her mouth was dry. 'So what you're saying is —'

'Yes!' Sam had an odd little smile on her face. 'It was one of us. Someone at the playgroup killed Barbara.'

The table fell silent. Everyone eyed each other.

'Or Lila,' said Eva, flicking her straight brown hair. 'She left early. She could have done it, come back in, waited a bit so it wasn't suspicious, and then legged it. You know she and Barbara don't get on.'

'Yes, but that doesn't mean she'd kill her.' Nick said, reasonably.

'She's got a temper, though.' Eva folded her arms.

'Or what about Imogen?' said Sam. 'She got banned last time. She might have got in, hidden somewhere, done it, and sneaked off.'

'How?' said Caitlin. 'First she'd have to get in without anyone seeing — OK, maybe she crept in when Barbara's back was turned — oh, sorry.' She bit her lip. 'But where would she hide? The toy cupboard's tiny, and people are in

55

and out of the loo all the time. The police will have checked the kitchen. And she couldn't have done it and left before we arrived, because we all saw Barbara alive at the start of playgroup.'

'Well, what about you?' Sam leaned forward. 'Barbara got your conservatory rejected, didn't she? You were hopping mad.'

'Don't be ridiculous!' snapped Caitlin.

'Calm down, everyone.' Nick made a shushing motion. 'Please.' He looked round the table. 'Barbara wound up a lot of people. Probably we all had a reason to be angry with her. But flinging accusations won't help. Let the police handle it.'

'Well, there's one person who didn't have a reason.' Caitlin turned towards Pippa. 'You've just moved here.' She paused, considering. 'Ooh, unless you're a long-lost relative with a grudge . . .'

'Do pack it in, Caitlin,' Nick said, wearily.

'Come on, Nick, I was joking.' Caitlin sipped her white wine. 'You can't blame me for trying to lighten the mood a bit.'

'Like I said, leave it to the police.' Nick drank his pint, a lowering expression on his face.

'Are we in trouble, Daddy?' Grace stared at him, a red crayon in her hand.

'No, sweetheart, no-one's in trouble. The police are just doing their job,' Nick said, in a soothing voice. 'What are you drawing?' He leaned over, and the muscles in his jaw tightened. Pippa glanced towards the sheet of paper. It showed a stick figure wearing a triangle for a skirt and a jumper made of loop-the-loops, with a sword sticking out of its tummy, spurting blood.

56

Pippa's eyes met Nick's. 'I guess it's — imaginative,' she faltered.

'You could say that,' Nick said grimly.

'Are you all ready to order?' Pippa wondered how long the barman had been standing there. 'Now, would anyone like a starter?'

Pippa looked at the mix of anger, confusion, and resentment around the table. 'I think we'll go straight to main.'

CHAPTER 10

'Come on, pick up the damn phone,' Pippa muttered, rescuing Freddie's toothbrush from the plughole and putting it in the mug. Freddie himself was napping, having eaten roughly his own bodyweight of sausages and beans at the pub, followed by a good go in the playground.

'You have reached Simon Parker's phone . . .'

Pippa pressed *End Call*. She'd already left two messages.

Someone got murdered at playgroup this morning, she texted. If that didn't make him call, well . . .

Her phone rang five minutes later. 'Pippa, what's going on?'

'I told you. Someone was murdered. At playgroup. While we were in the hall.'

'What, you mean you saw it?'

'No, no, it was in the kitchen. I went to help at snack time and we found her there.'

'Oh God, who was it? Not one of the kids?'

'No, the playgroup leader. Someone called Barbara. Barbara Hamilton.'

'Barbara Hamilton?' Simon sounded incredulous.

'Do you remember her?'

'She's one of Mum's friends. Oh heck. Does Mum know?'

'I doubt it, it was this morning.'

'She'll be in pieces when she hears. I'd better phone and tell her before someone else does.' Pause. 'You're sure it was murder?'

'The police said so. She'd had her head bashed in. But you probably shouldn't tell your mum that bit.'

'Oh God. Are you all right?'

Pippa paused. 'I think so. It's just . . .'

'What? I can't stay on long, I'm meant to be on a comfort break.'

'It was someone from the playgroup.'

'Are you sure?'

'It's a classic locked-room mystery. No one could have got in or out without being seen, and there's nowhere to hide.'

'That's speculation. Look, I must go now. I'll come home tomorrow. I'll tell Declan you're having contractions, or something.'

'Thanks.'

'Oh, Pippa, will you phone Mum and tell her the news for me? I'm a bit busy.'

'It would be better coming from you.' Pippa said firmly.

'Hmm. Maybe you're right,' Simon sighed. 'How is Mum, anyway? I had a chat with her last night. She seemed a bit tired.'

'I don't know, we haven't spoken.'

'Oh Pippa. I thought you'd have gone to visit her by now. It's not as if she's far away.'

'Why can't she visit me? I could use the help. I'm

VERY PREGNANT, remember?'

Silence, then Simon sighed again. 'I have to go. I'll see you tomorrow.'

'When?'

'I'll text. Bye now, Pippa.'

'Bye.'

Pippa put the phone on the sink, although she would have liked to throw it at the wall. The only things stopping her were firstly that she needed the phone, and secondly that, knowing her luck, it would make a hole in both the wall and their deposit. *Hmmm*, she thought. *I should chase up the estate agent.*

Someone answered on the third ring. 'Scarisbrick Jones, Nessa speaking.'

'Oh, er, um, I'm calling to check on progress with a house sale.'

'Who's calling, please?'

'This is Pippa Parker.'

'Oh yes, Mrs Parker. And which house was it?' Nessa chirped.

'Laurel Villa. Oh, and I'm reporting an issue with the water supply.'

'At Laurel Villa?' Nessa sounded suspicious now.

'No, at Rosebud Cottage. The one we're renting while Laurel Villa goes through.'

'I'll transfer you,' Nessa said frostily. A click, followed by beeping.

'Scarisbrick Jones, Eric speaking.'

'Hi, it's Pippa Parker.'

'And what can I do for you today, Mrs Parker?' Eric's voice was cheery. Pippa wished it were possible to punch someone down the phone.

'Hasn't Nessa told you why I'm calling?'

'I always like to hear it from the client, Mrs Parker.'

Pippa gritted her teeth and explained it again.

'Oh I *see*. Yes. Let me get the file.' Rapid typing. 'Laurel Villa — here we are. Yes, everything's progressing.'

'So the owners are ready to exchange?'

'It's progressing as expected,' said Eric, a little less smugly.

'What does that mean? Have they found somewhere else? Are they ready to move?'

'Mrs Parker, that is confidential information.'

'All right, can you give me a date?'

'Not as yet, Mrs Parker, but —'

'An approximate date?'

'We don't like to deal in approximations, Mrs Parker. I'd rather wait and confirm a definite date with you when we have more information.'

Pippa nearly growled. 'In that case, I'd like to report a problem with the water supply.'

'At Laurel Villa?'

'No!' Pippa remembered Freddie and took a deep breath. 'At Rosebud Cottage.'

'Oh?'

'The cottage we're renting while Laurel Villa completes.' Pippa gritted her teeth.

'Oh yes.' More typing. 'What sort of problem?'

'The water has bits in it. I can't tell if it's safe to drink. I'm boiling it.'

'That would be a matter for the water company —'

'It's not just that.' Pippa interrupted before Eric got into full flow. 'The roof leaks, and there's damp. It seriously

61

needs looking at. Could you speak to the landlord for me?'

'Yes. Yes, I'll send them an email and see if they'll authorise repairs.'

'Er, they'd better.' Pippa gripped the edge of the sink. 'I'm not entirely sure this house is fit to live in.'

'It's not as simple as that, Mrs Parker,' said Eric. 'Rosebud Cottage is a listed building. We can't send any old person in. They have to be approved. Otherwise the council would come after us.'

'Well, maybe they'll come after you when I report this place to Environmental Health —'

'Calm down, Mrs Parker.' Now Pippa really wanted to punch him. 'As I said, I'll send the landlord an email —'

'You won't! You'll phone them!'

'Yes, I'll phone them. Don't worry, Mrs Parker, we will deal with it. *Beep*. Now, I have someone on the other line. Goodbye, Mrs Parker.' The phone cut off.

Pippa took aim at the wall opposite, then slowly lowered her arm. She was breathing hard and fast, and her heart pounded. *Calm down, Pippa. For the baby.* She bowed her head and breathed deeply until her heartbeat had slowed to something like normal. Right. Simon was coming home tomorrow. He could help sort things out. 'Yes,' she said grimly. 'You can do your bit, Simon Parker.'

She checked the time on her phone. Just after four o'clock. If she hurried, she could start off a chicken stew before Freddie woke. It had definitely been a chicken stew sort of day. A day that had begun with a murder, and got worse.

Pippa crept downstairs, avoiding the creaky floorboard, and went into the tiny kitchen. Chicken pieces, stock cube, casserole dish, onions, carrots, she recited to herself. She turned on the tap to wash her hands.

After some thumping, water flowed.

Better wait for it to warm up. She leaned against the worktop, surveying the front garden. The lawn was patchy, and the leaves on the bushes were brown and drooping. She wrinkled her nose. Those bushes definitely weren't listed.

Pippa put her hand under the tap, and flinched. It was icy cold. She checked the taps. No, that was definitely the hot tap. As an experiment, she turned it off and tried the cold tap, which was warmer but still by no definition hot.

Pippa went upstairs and turned on the taps in the bathroom, with the same result.

No hot water.

Wait — perhaps the boiler —

Where was the boiler?

After a thorough search Pippa found the boiler hidden in one of the wall units in the kitchen. The pilot light was on, and the nearest radiator was warm. How was it possible to have heating but no hot water? She picked up her phone and pressed *Redial*.

'Scarisbrick Jones, Nessa speaking.'

'Hello Nessa, it's Pippa Parker again. I now have no hot water.'

'One second, Mrs Parker.' Pippa focused on composing herself while the hold beeps sounded. 'Have you tried running the tap?'

Pippa took a deep breath. 'Yes, I have tried running all the taps.'

More hold beeps. 'Have you checked the boiler, Mrs Parker?'

63

'Yes,' said Pippa through gritted teeth. 'I have checked the boiler, and it is working. And the radiators are working too.'

'I'll send a message to the landlord for you, Mrs Parker —'

'Please phone the landlord, Nessa.'

'Of course, Mrs Parker,' sing-songed Nessa. 'I'll get on to that right away. Thank you, Mrs Parker.'

A quarter past four on a Thursday afternoon. Pippa calculated the odds of Nessa doing anything about her call before tomorrow, and multiplied that by the chances of someone coming out to Rosebud Cottage before the weekend. Slim to none was her closest approximation. She filled the kettle and flicked the switch, and her mouth set. Well, let Simon come and experience the delights of rural life this weekend. Washing in an inch of water, wearing three jumpers, and living out of boxes. *I'll probably never see him again*, she thought, and wondered why she wasn't more bothered by the prospect.

CHAPTER 11

'Pippa!'

'Simon! I didn't think you'd be — why didn't you text me?'

'I did.' Simon walked towards her. 'Didn't you get it?'

'Daddy!' Freddie rushed towards Simon and hugged his knees. 'Pick up!'

Simon swung him into the air. 'Freddie! I've missed you! And I've got a present for you, in my suitcase.' He waved a hand at his car, parked some distance from the trees.

'Ooo! What? What?' He put Freddie down and walked to the gate, Freddie toddling after him on his little legs. Pippa surreptitiously pulled her phone from her pocket and checked her messages. Nothing. She turned to the window she had been cleaning and wiped away a smear.

'Don't I get a kiss?' Simon wheeled his case towards her, with Freddie bouncing beside him.

'Of course you do,' Pippa said automatically. Simon hugged her awkwardly with his free arm and gave her a peck on the cheek.

'I got the first train, and a taxi from the station.' Simon

kept his arm round her. 'But I had to bring some work home.'

'Uh-huh,' said Pippa. She pushed the door open.

'Oi!'

The sudden shout made Simon stand upright, and he whacked his head on the doorframe. 'Sh — oops!'

'The Prodigal Son returns!' Marge stumped towards them.

'Good grief — Marge!' Simon bounded over to her. 'How are you? And how's the apple tree?'

'All the better for your absence,' said Marge, reaching up and ruffling his hair. 'You've grown a bit since we last met, Master Parker.'

'And you've shrunk a bit,' Simon grinned. Beyoncé dashed over and threw herself on the path at his feet, writhing, and meowing.

'Cheeky animal,' Marge commented. 'Well, I'll leave you young lovebirds to it. If you want to drop round for a cuppa, you know where I am.' She raised a hand in salute, and stomped off, rocking from side to side like a sailor on an unsteady boat.

'She hasn't changed a bit,' said Simon. 'Nor have you, Pippa.' He gave her a proper kiss this time. 'Except Bump has grown even bigger.' He stepped back and examined her critically. 'When's your due date again?'

'Five weeks. Ish. I can't remember, exactly.' Pippa frowned. 'Oh heck, baby brain.'

'You don't look as if you're going to last five weeks. What's that in your hand?' He tugged at the cloth, then prodded the bucket nearby with his foot. 'Should you be doing that in your condition?'

'Well, It isn't as if I've had anyone else to do it.' Simon

raised his eyebrows. 'I'm not being snarky,' she said. 'It's just how it's been.'

'Mm.' His eyes narrowed. 'Are you nesting?'

'I don't know! I'm cleaning things that need cleaning!'

'Present! Present!' Freddie tugged on Simon's hand, clearly feeling the conversation was going on the wrong track.

'Let's get you inside.' Simon put his hand on her back in a proprietorial way that made her want to shake him off. 'Then you can have your present, Freddie.'

'Yayyyyyyy!' Freddie ran ahead, tripped over the doorstep, and thunked onto the floor. A wail rose into the air.

'You pick him up,' Pippa said to Simon. 'I'm sure he's fine.'

Simon hurried ahead, scooped Freddie from the floor, and kissed the bit of Freddie's head that he was rubbing. 'There, there, Freddie. Let's sit you on the sofa and get your present.'

'What sofa?' said Pippa. 'It wouldn't fit, remember?'

'Oh.' Simon put Freddie down, lifted a box of DVDs from the armchair, and put him into it. 'There we go.' He went outside for his case, brought it in, and opened it. Pippa glimpsed a tangled heap of shirts and socks and boxers.

'I didn't have time to pack properly,' said Simon, catching Pippa's look.

'What did Declan say about you coming home early?'

'Oh, he was fine. Said family had to come first, and all that.' Simon rummaged around the case, pulling a brightly-coloured box from the bottom left. 'Here you are, Freddie!' He put it into Freddie's hands. 'A digger!'

67

'Wow!' shouted Freddie, ripping into the box and pulling at the bright yellow plastic.

'Hang on Freddie, let me get it out for you,' Pippa said.

'I can do it!' Freddie said, holding it away from her.

'I don't think you can — see, there are cable ties. We need scissors.' She prised the box from Freddie's hands and went to the kitchen drawer. Behind her, an aggrieved sniff.

Simon followed her into the kitchen. 'This is smaller than I remembered,' he said, jerking a thumb at the door.

'Yes, and crappier.' Pippa found the scissors and worked a blade under the first cable tie. 'There's no hot water now.'

'Really? Have you checked the boiler?' Simon began opening cupboards.

'Yes,' growled Pippa. 'I may be pregnant, but I'm not stupid.'

'I'll phone the estate agent.'

'I already did that.' Pippa put the scissors down in case she stabbed him. But Simon was already scrolling down his phone. He held it to his ear and wandered off.

'I give up,' Pippa said to the kitchen clock. She cut the remaining cable tie, marched into the sitting room, and put the digger on Freddie's lap. He beamed at it, not at her. 'Thank you, Mummy, for sorting out my toy. That's quite all right, Freddie.' Simon was strolling outside. His free hand, finger pointed, was slicing the air in an I-am-making-a-point sort of way.

Simon came back in, looking smug. 'They're sending someone round this afternoon.'

'What?' Pippa's mouth dropped open. 'But I rang them yesterday and they kept putting me off!'

68

'Ah, well,' Simon put the phone in his pocket with a little smile. 'Shall I help you get this place straight?'

Pippa's eyes roamed over the half-unpacked boxes, the carrier bags stuffed in the corner, and the dusty mantelpiece. 'That would be great,' she admitted.

'Well, there's only so much you can do.' Simon straightened a picture with his index finger. 'When are you seeing the midwife?' His voice was casual.

'Mmm. I suppose I should register with the doctor . . .'

Simon looked horrified. 'Yes, you should!'

'All right, all right! It's just with all the stuff to do, and the m —', she jerked her head at Freddie.

'Put your feet up,' said Simon, clearing another armchair. 'I'll get you a cup of tea.'

'I'm not an invalid,' Pippa protested. But it was nice to sit down, and have a cushion plumped, and a box brought for a footstool.

'You deserve a rest,' called Simon. 'Anyway, the house needs a good going-over before Mum sees it.'

Alarm bells rang in Pippa's head. 'And when is Sheila going to be seeing it?'

'I invited her for lunch tomorrow,' Simon shouted from the kitchen. 'I thought it would cheer her up, what with the news about Barbara.'

'Did you.' Pippa wondered if rocketing blood pressure could induce labour and release her from this nightmare.

'Yes, and it worked. She stopped crying and everything. I said we'd cook roast lamb, that's her favourite.'

'You do realise I don't know how to cook on the range?' Pippa uncurled her fists. 'Unless she likes it either raw or burnt to a crisp.'

'We can work it out between us,' said Simon cheerily,

69

bringing in a cup of tea.

'Mm.' Pippa put her head back and took deep breaths.

'You're not having a contraction, are you?' Simon demanded. 'Although after what I told Declan —'

'What did you tell Declan?'

'Oh, that you were having panic attacks.'

'Thanks very much.' Pippa sipped her tea. 'No, I'm not having a contraction. Or a panic attack. I'm annoyed that you invited your mother round without checking with me first.'

'Come on Pippa, she's had a terrible shock. At her age, that's a big thing. I thought making a fuss of her might take her mind off it a bit.'

Pippa looked at the box her feet had been on, then at the cup of tea. Her cushion seemed to grow plumper. 'Is that what you're doing with me? Making a fuss so I put up with this bloody house, and your mother?'

'Pippa!' Simon jerked his head towards Freddie.

Pippa stood, with difficulty. 'I don't care! I've had a miserable week, and if this is what it's going to be like, I don't want to live here!'

'Pippa, you don't mean it —' Simon walked towards her.

'Oh yes I do!' Pippa shook off the hand he laid on her arm. 'The only normal people I've met so far are from the playgroup — and one of them's a murderer! I mean, what the f —' She got her coat from the banister and slung the changing bag over her shoulder, then thought better of it. She took out her purse and keys, and dropped the bag on the floor. 'I'll see you later.'

'P —'

BANG. The letterbox rattled as she slammed the front

door.

There. That felt better. Pippa stuck her hands in her pockets and walked away from the house.

'Trouble in paradise?' cackled Marge through the open window. Pippa ignored her and whistled as she walked down River Lane and turned right into the village. *Face up to your responsibilities, Simon.* She smiled. *It's about bloody time.*

CHAPTER 12

Pippa had got as far as the village green when her phone rang. That was a quick turnaround. She dug in her pocket with grim satisfaction.

But it wasn't Simon. The number was unfamiliar; not a mobile number, which in itself was strange. Pippa braced herself for a conversation about PPI or a new conservatory, and pressed *Accept*.

'Hello, is that Mrs Parker?' A man's voice, older than her, and probably local.

'It is. Who's calling?'

'This is Inspector Fanshawe from Gadcestershire Police. It's in connection with the incident at . . . Gadding Goslings playgroup.' He pronounced the words carefully. Pippa imagined it wasn't something in his usual line of work. 'I'm at Much Gadding police station today. Are you available to give a statement and answer some questions?' By the end he sounded much more sure of himself. It was an instruction, not a request.

'Yes, I can come down.'

'Are you busy at the moment, Mrs Parker? I could fit you in now.'

Pippa reluctantly shelved the idea of a cup of tea and a cream cake. 'Yes, if you like.' The cream cake was merely postponed. It would be her reward. 'Where is the police station?'

'It's by St Saviour's Church, on the Greater Gadding road. I'll expect you in a few minutes, Mrs Parker.' And the Inspector rang off.

Pippa took a few deep breaths before making her way to the police station. It was a tiny pebble-dashed cube, a blue lamp the only notification of its purpose. A board outside carried warnings about leaving cars unlocked and the penalties for littering. What were they making of this? She pushed the door open, and went in.

PC Horsley was sitting behind the counter, his face lit by the glow of a computer monitor. 'Good morning, Mrs Parker. Do take a seat.' He indicated two plastic chairs set against the wall. 'The Inspector will be with you in a moment.' He resumed typing.

'How long do you think this will take?'

PC Horsley had to half-stand to see her. 'Difficult to say, Mrs Parker. It depends what you have to tell us.'

'There isn't much, Constable Horsley.'

'Perhaps twenty minutes.'

Pippa pulled out her phone. *Have been called in to give statement to police*, she texted. *Will let you know if I'm arrested.*

'Switch that off, please.' PC Horsley admonished.

Pippa pressed *Send* and then did as she was told. It would do Simon good for her to be unreachable for a bit.

The door to the back room swung open and a foxy-looking man in uniform appeared. 'Mrs Parker? I'm Inspector Fanshawe. Would you like to come through?'

73

Pippa began the slow process of getting to her feet. 'Take your time,' said the Inspector, his eyes on Pippa's bump.

The back room had been hastily adapted for interviewing. One of the desks had been cleared for use as a table, and two swivel chairs and a plastic chair were placed round it. A tidy kitchenette stood in the corner, and film posters (mostly police chase dramas) covered the walls. 'Do take a seat, Mrs Parker,' said the Inspector, indicating the plastic chair.

'Thank you.' Pippa sat down, and the Inspector sat opposite, oscillating slightly.

'I'll join you in a moment, once I've closed up,' said PC Horsley.

Did this really need two of them? Pippa began to cross her legs before realising that with the bump, it was far too much effort.

PC Horsley returned, shutting the door with a click. He fetched a laptop from the uncleared desk and sat in the other swivel chair, beside the Inspector. 'I'll be typing your statement as we go, Mrs Parker. I'll ask you to read the printout and sign it at the end.'

Pippa nodded, hot and guilty. She racked her brains for anything she might have done, but apart from driving at 32 miles an hour in a 30 mph area, she was blank. And she'd done the speed awareness course, anyway.

The Inspector smiled faintly as PC Horsley frowned, and clicked, and pursed his mouth at the screen. 'All right, good to go.'

Inspector Fanshawe's smile broadened to general encouragement. 'So, we would like you to tell us, in your own words, everything you can about what happened on the morning of Thursday 13th October. We may ask you some questions to clarify what you have said. It is perfectly all right to say that you don't know the answer. However, I must stress that you are expected to tell the truth, and this statement will be admissible as evidence in court. Do you agree to this, Mrs Parker?'

'I do,' Pippa had a little flashback of herself standing next to Simon in church, and set her mouth firmly to keep it from twitching.

'Interview and witness statement with Mrs Parker, Friday 14th October 2016. To begin, Mrs Parker, please can you confirm your full name.'

'Philippa Jane Parker,' Pippa said. Her voice seemed much louder than usual.

'And your maiden name?'

'Smith.'

'Your age and date of birth, please.'

'Twenty-nine. The seventh of March, 1987. *Stand By Me* was number one in the charts.'

'Don't record that last bit, PC Horsley.' The Inspector looked Pippa straight in the eye. 'May I remind you this is evidence, Mrs Parker.'

'Yes, sorry, Inspector. Just a bit nervous.'

'That's fine. Try to relax.' The Inspector and PC Horsley exchanged glances.

PC Horsley leaned forward. 'Place of interview, Much Gadding Police Station. Also present, Inspector T Fanshawe and Police Constable J Horsley. Time commenced,' — he glanced at his wrist — 'ten forty-six.'

The Inspector swivelled a little. 'Right, Mrs Parker, in your own words, please.'

'Er, where should I start?'

'Perhaps from your arrival at playgroup that morning?

When did you arrive?'

'I was five minutes early, so five to ten. I'd walked down with Lila. The church hall was already open, and people were there.'

'So — Lila — came to your house? From that point, then, please.'

Pippa gave her account, accompanied by PC Horsley on the laptop, to the point where the policeman had arrived at the playgroup.

'Mm.' The Inspector gazed at a poster of *The Fugitive* for some seconds. A printer chattered in the corner. 'I understand you are new to the village, Mrs Parker.' He drew a notebook from his pocket.

'Yes, I moved in on Monday.'

'And you are in the process of buying a house?' Pippa realised with a shock that the policemen had already discussed her.

'That's right, yes.'

'Did you know anyone from Much Gadding prior to moving here?'

'My mother-in-law.'

'And she is..?'

'Mrs Sheila Parker.'

'That name's familiar, sir,' broke in PC Horsley. 'She's phoned a few times to complain about noisy neighbours. I have her details on file.'

The Inspector made a note. 'And did she know Mrs Hamilton?'

'Yes, they were friends.'

'Has your mother-in-law lived in Much Gadding for a long time?'

'Yes, my husband grew up here, so that must be thirty

76

years or more.'

'And your husband's name?'

'Simon Parker.' Another note.

'And does Mr Parker live with you?'

'Yes, but he works away a lot.' Pippa paused. 'I don't see where this is going.'

'Just establishing a bit of background, Mrs Parker. It's useful to connect people.' The Inspector put his elbows on the desk and steepled his fingers. 'Now, did anyone at the playgroup seem different from usual, before the incident was discovered?'

Pippa thought. 'Not particularly. I've only met most of them once, at the playgroup on Tuesday. People were a bit less anxious, I suppose.'

'That's interesting. Can you think of a reason?'

'Honestly?' Pippa smiled. 'Probably because Barbara was out of the room for most of the time.'

'So would you say that her presence caused tension?'

Pippa considered. 'Yes. At the Tuesday playgroup, she banned someone. They'd brought a plastic toy and she didn't like them. She said they were pollutants.'

PC Horsley snorted, then subsided under a glance from the Inspector.

'I see.' The Inspector put his chin on his steepled fingers for a moment. 'And was that person at playgroup on Thursday?'

'No. Barbara hadn't said whether she'd allow her back.'

'Mm. Do you happen to know whether anyone else might hold a grudge against Mrs Hamilton?'

Pippa recalled the conversation round the table in the pub. 'I can't remember who said what, exactly, but the impression I got was that Barbara had annoyed quite a few people. Refusing planning permission, making sure kids didn't get into the local primary school. That sort of thing.' She looked up at the Inspector, worried that she had gone too far. But she had promised to tell the whole truth.

The Inspector held her gaze until Pippa wriggled in her chair. 'Yes,' he said, eventually. 'That information does fit with what we've heard from other witnesses, though you put it rather more tactfully. Is there anything else you'd like to tell us, Mrs Parker?'

'I can't think of anything.' Pippa felt as if she'd been turned inside out and given a good shake.

'If we do have any further questions, we'll be in touch. Now, do you have any questions for us?'

'Only the sort of questions you can't answer. Like who did it.'

'Quite.' The Inspector flashed her a wintry smile. 'Oh, one more thing.' His eyes slid towards PC Horsley.

'Yes. Can we take your fingerprints, Mrs Parker?'

Pippa flinched. 'What, you mean now? Actual fingerprints?' she stammered.

The Inspector leaned forward, smiling like a favourite uncle. 'Don't worry, Mrs Parker, we're asking everyone. It's routine.'

Pippa swallowed. 'What if I say no?'

'We won't force you,' Inspector Fanshawe remarked, mildly. 'However, refusing wouldn't look very good, would it?'

Pippa blinked, and bit her lip. 'All right,' she muttered.

'Excellent.' The Inspector brought over a small scanner. 'One finger at a time, please. Are you right or left-handed?'

'Right.'

Out of the corner of her eye, Pippa saw PC Horsley

make a note, then go to the printer. He returned with a few sheets of paper, putting them in front of her. 'Can you read this, Mrs Parker. If you're happy with it, sign each sheet at the bottom, and again in the box at the end.'

Once the scanner had beeped its last, and the Inspector had taken it away, Pippa did as she was told, feeling sick as she turned the pages. It all seemed so small and trivial, and yet, behind the serving hatch, someone had killed Barbara Hamilton. She reached for the pen which PC Horsley had slid across the table, and scrawled her signature. 'What happens now?' she asked, warily.

'We investigate,' said the Inspector, sitting back. 'This is likely to be a difficult case, with multiple suspects. Plus we don't have anyone with extensive local knowledge.'

'What about the policeman who retired?' Pippa asked. 'Norman, was it? Someone mentioned him.'

'Oh, Norm,' snorted PC Horsley. 'He was more interested in doing safety talks than any actual detective work.'

'A good local copper, though,' commented the Inspector, raising his eyebrows.

'Oh yes, sir,' PC Horsley agreed hastily.

'Can I go now?' asked Pippa.

'Of course, Mrs Parker. PC Horsley, would you mind seeing Mrs Parker out?'

'Sir.' PC Horsley stood and led the way from the room without a word to Pippa. A loud knock sounded on the door. 'Someone's keen,' said the policeman, half-jocularly. He drew the bolt and pulled the door open, and Simon half-fell into the station.

'What have you been playing at, Pippa?' He looked more angry than Pippa had ever seen him, and it didn't suit him one bit. More angry than didn't-win-the-contract angry, or lost-the-league angry.

'Excuse me?' Pippa made to step back, but Simon grabbed her by the arm and marched her off. 'Where's Freddie?'

'I left him with Marge.' Simon's grip pinched her arm.

'Will you let go of me!' Pippa shook him off. 'What's up with you?'

'I've just spent the last twenty minutes on the phone to Mum, who is beside herself. She rang after you texted her saying you might be arrested.'

'What? I didn't text her, I texted you.'

'No you didn't,' Simon said through gritted teeth. 'It's one thing to have a row with me, but not to take it out on my mum.'

Pippa switched her phone on. *Sent Messages*. And there it was, sent not to Simon, but Sheila.

'Oh bollocks.'

'You idiot, Pippa.'

'It was a mistake!' Pippa cried. 'And if you think — oh, what's the point.' She pushed past him and stomped up the path, trying not to wipe her eyes too obviously. The police probably thought she was married to a psychopath now. Ha, maybe they'd pull him in for questioning.

Pippa paused at the village green, and sat on a bench. She didn't fancy a trip to the tearoom now; in fact the thought of a cream cake turned her stomach. If anything, she wanted somewhere quiet. She gazed across the green for inspiration, and found it. A little sign squashed in between the bakery and the country store. *Library*.

Pippa heaved herself up, and walked towards it.

CHAPTER 13

The library was possibly even smaller on the inside than it appeared from the green. A tiny vestibule with all the familiar flyers led to a room with three walls of books, and a small desk at the far end where someone was reading a newspaper. Pippa judged that security wasn't exactly high. Then again, she thought, inspecting the shelves, the books wouldn't be high on a thief's list. Most of them were considerably older than her.

She wandered forward, scanning the shelves. Aha! She selected *The Body In The Library*, *Murder at the Vicarage*, and *A Murder Is Announced*, and approached the desk.

'How do I become a member?' she asked the newspaper.

It lowered, slowly, revealing a broad, grey-haired man. 'You write your name, address and phone number in this book.' He pushed forward a black ledger. 'Then you give me your books, and I make a note in *this* book.' He patted a red ledger. 'And there you go.'

'Don't I need a library card or something?'

'Nah.' The man put down his newspaper. 'We're not an official sort of library. Now, what have you chosen?' Pippa put her books on the desk, the spines towards him. 'Ah! Very good, very good. Mind you, I do find Miss Marple's habit of comparing everyone to a person she once knew somewhat wearying.'

Pippa smiled. 'You're not a fan?'

The man looked shocked. 'Oh, I'm a huge fan. But I prefer Poirot myself. Read 'em all. Wonderful practice for work, you see.'

'For work . . . ?' Pippa scrutinised the man. 'Are you . . . ?'

'I used to be the village policeman, till I took early retirement.' The man's eyes twinkled. 'I decided I'd had enough of chopping and changing to suit whatever fashion of policing was in this year. And when they asked me to cover three villages for the same money, I said my goodbyes and drew my pension with gratitude.'

'Your name's Norm, isn't it?'

'That's right.' Norm extended a large reddish hand. 'And you are?'

'Pippa. Pippa Parker.' Pippa shook the hand. 'I've just moved here.'

'Ah, then you probably haven't heard the big news in the village.' Norm leaned across the desk.

'Do you mean . . . the murder?'

Norm rubbed his hands. 'Ooh, I'd love to get involved, but that young hound Horsley won't let me within a yard of the place. Like any dog, he's got his own patch to protect.' He eyed Pippa curiously. 'So how do you know?'

'I was there, with my toddler.'

'No!' Norm gasped. 'Oh, what I'd give to have been a fly on the wall!'

'I'm pretty sure I'm not meant to discuss it,' said Pippa.

'I didn't see anything, anyway. It all happened offstage, so to speak.'

'Those are the best kind of murders!' Norm cried. 'And tell me, was it a locked-room affair?'

'The kind where only the people in the building could have done it?'

Norm nodded eagerly.

'Well, it was at the church hall, and all the exits are in the room we were in, so —'

'Oh, I've dreamed of a murder like that happening on my patch!' His mouth turned down. 'I imagine I'll be following it in the newspapers, though.'

'So did you know her?' Pippa asked, cautiously.

'Course I did! Known her — well, *knew* her, I should say — since she moved to the village.'

'Oh, I thought she'd always lived here. She seemed like that sort of person.'

'No, she'd been here for the last, what, ten years maybe? Although the way time passes these days . . . But she threw herself into village life, did Barbara. A little too much, if you ask me. I think she wanted to leave her stamp on it.' Norm paused. 'And by golly, she did.'

'Did you like her?'

Norm frowned. 'I tried,' he said, eventually. 'She did a lot of good. I admired that. But, well, I never felt it was to *do* good, as such. It was more that she wanted to be known for doing it.' He mused. 'Funny things, people.' Suddenly he snapped to attention. 'Anyway, your books. Pop your name in my big black book, now, and I'll write these in the other one.'

'Do you need to see them again?'

Norm tapped his head. 'All in here. Policeman's

memory. Like an elephant, I am.' He watched Pippa write in the book. 'And if anything springs to mind . . . pay me a visit, won't you.'

Pippa grinned. She liked Norm, with his air of being somehow outside, looking in. 'I'll probably be back soon for more books. I'm a fast reader.'

'Good. We like those.'

Pippa walked home with her books. Time to face the music. She still felt angry and resentful, but her anger was starting to wear off. Given the misunderstanding, she could see why Simon had been furious. It had been a pretty flippant text to send, but it wasn't her fault it had gone to Sheila by mistake. Unless Simon thought it was some sort of joke. He should know her better than that. Pippa felt the anger rising again — or was it heartburn? — and choked it down. She crossed the road by the war memorial and headed towards River Lane. Two figures were ahead of her, standing on the river bank. A little one and a big one. Simon and Freddie? She quickened her pace, with a pang of guilt that she hadn't missed Freddie at all since she had flounced out of the house earlier.

'Freddie!' she cried.

The little figure waved a sort of stick. 'Mummy!' But who was that with him?

'Ah, Pippa!' boomed from the taller figure. Marge. Of course. 'We've been fishing!'

'Look, Mummy! Phone! In the water!' Freddie pointed to the ground with what Pippa now saw was a net. Sure enough, a grubby old mobile lay on the bank.

'Wow, well done!' She turned to Marge, who was grinning broadly. 'Thank you for minding Freddie.'

'Oh, we've had a great time. Haven't we, Freddie?'

84

'Yeah!' Freddie shouted. 'Can we fish, Mummy? Can I keep it?'

'Maybe,' said Pippa, automatically. 'We should probably see if it works first, and try and find the owner.' Freddie's lip stuck out. 'I could get you a toy phone . . .'

'Yay!' He jumped up and down.

'Come to bury the hatchet?' said Marge, smiling.

Pippa sighed. 'I suppose so.'

Marge beckoned Pippa closer and whispered in her ear. 'Well, you've got a stay of execution. Your husband said he was going shopping, and then to visit his mum. He didn't say when he'd be back.' She turned and bellowed to Freddie. 'Come on, young man. Time to clean your catch and hand you over to your mum.' Freddie came running up. 'I've given him lunch, he seemed peckish,' she muttered to Pippa. 'Good eater, isn't he?'

'Oh yes,' said Pippa. 'Thank you ever so much, Marge.' Suddenly she had to blink, hard.

'That's all right, dear. Now Freddie, why don't you run on ahead to the house and see if you can find Beyoncé outside.' Freddie bounced off, shrieking in a way that would scare any cat for miles around. 'If you don't mind me saying . . .'

Pippa braced herself for a lecture on wifely duty.

'That husband of yours should be here looking after you, not zooming off in his company car being a hot-shot executive. That's what I told him, anyway.'

Oh God.

'You put the boy down for a nap and have a rest, that's my advice. I understand someone's coming to check your water. I'll watch for 'em, and I've got a spare key.'

'Thanks Marge, but you don't have to —'

'You look like you need a break.' Marge scooped up Freddie's booty with her net. 'How *do* you get a phone working when it's been in water?'

'You put it in rice,' said Pippa.

Marge stared as if she'd grown an extra head. 'What, any rice? Or a particular kind?' She held the net out to Pippa.

'Any kind.' Pippa extracted the dripping phone.

'Well, now,' said Marge. 'Every day's a school day. What have you got there?' She gestured at Pippa's armful of books.

'I joined the library,' said Pippa. 'Norm was on duty.'

'Jolly good,' said Marge, peering at the books. 'Ooh, I do love a good juicy murder. You go and get stuck in. Have you found her, young man?' she bellowed.

Freddie was lying flat on the ground with his arm stretched under a bush. 'Cat-cat!' he shouted.

'She's not daft, that cat,' muttered Marge. 'And don't worry about your husband. He'll be fine once he's let off steam.'

'Mm,' Pippa agreed. But as she gathered up Freddie and his belongings, she wished she could believe it.

CHAPTER 14

Pippa tweaked a cushion into place as Freddie ran across the room and dived into the armchair. 'Freddie! Grandma will be here in a minute!'

'Sorry,' came a muffled voice from the depths of the armchair.

Pippa surveyed the room. She had to admit that unpacking all the boxes had made a big difference. The place was crammed with things, but it did at least look like home.

Simon had come home at half-past five the day before. As soon as Freddie heard his key in the front door, he dropped his new digger and ran to him. 'Daddy! Don't go again!' Simon put down his shopping bags, picked Freddie up and ruffled his hair. 'Well, Daddy has to go to work, Freddie,' he said in a reasonable voice.

Pippa met Simon's eye. He put Freddie down and picked the bags up again. 'I'd better get all this put away.'

'I'll help,' said Pippa, uncurling herself from the armchair and following him into the kitchen. 'How's Sheila?' she asked in a low voice, as she stacked tins in the cupboard.

Simon didn't answer for a few moments, as he put milk and butter into the fridge. 'Once I'd explained the message was a joke and you meant to send it to me, she seemed better. Still not happy though.' He slid a pack of yogurts onto the top shelf. 'Quite cross with you.'

Pippa pushed a white bloomer loaf into the bread bin. 'Is that you, or her?'

'Both,' Simon said shortly, and banged the fridge door shut. 'Pippa, we have to make a go of this, and you stropping all over the place isn't helping at all.'

'How would you know? You've been in the village two minutes. You have no idea what it's like. How would you feel if you were chucked into a new environment a few weeks — A FEW WEEKS — before having a baby, and then you find out someone is a murderer?' Pippa paused to catch her breath. 'It's hardly the best start, is it? Especially in this pit.' She gestured at the kitchen, which, even after a good clean, was still markedly shabby.

'Did someone come about the hot water?' Simon switched the kettle on.

'Yes.' Pippa rubbed her forehead. 'He said it's an intermittent boiler fault. Anyway, the water's safe to drink. They tested it a few months ago for the last tenant.'

The boiler man had been surprisingly obliging. 'Wondered when I'd be round again,' he'd said, rummaging in his toolbox. 'This boiler's practically family, I visit it more often than my gran.'

'Is there any way you could say the boiler's unsafe, so I can get it replaced?'

He shook his head. 'It's the kind that grumbles along for years. I don't fancy your chances.' He took out a spanner and gave the boiler a good whack on the side. 'Try

88

now.'

Pippa snorted and turned the sink tap on. Within ten seconds the water was warm. 'So I just whack the boiler?'

He considered, arms folded. 'Well, I'm a fully qualified professional, so I bring years of training and expertise to my whacks. But yes, it's worth a try.' He took the pencil from behind his ear and drew a tiny cross on the side of the boiler. 'That's the sweet spot. You can have that for free.'

'Thanks,' said Pippa. 'Another cup of tea? That one's gone cold.'

He swirled the mug, and they watched the small brown particles skate over the surface. 'I'll give it a miss, thanks,' he said, closing his toolbox with a snap. 'On my way to the next one. I've no doubt I'll see you again.'

Pippa watched the man get into his van and drive away. Why was she sad to see him go? She stood for a moment, pondering the question. Probably because they had talked normally without the murder hanging over them, or the tension of the move. Well, at least Freddie could have a bath tonight. She crept upstairs and looked at him sleeping in his now-assembled cot. He was getting too big for it, but they had decided to wait until Laurel Villa to buy a proper bed. Waiting, waiting.

And now they were waiting for Sheila to arrive, and Freddie was getting increasingly hyperactive. 'When's Ganma coming?' He dived into the armchair again with a *whump*.

'Soon, Freddie, soon.'

Eventually Pippa heard the familiar sound of Simon's engine purring to a halt. 'They're here, Freddie.'

'Yeahhhh!' Freddie ran to the front door and stood by it in such a way that no-one would be able to get in.

'Calm down, Freddie.' Simon's voice issued from the gap which Freddie was attempting to insert himself into. 'And move back a bit, will you?'

With a final wriggle Freddie was through, and clinging to Sheila, who stroked his hair, looking helplessly at Simon.

'Freddie, let go,' said Pippa, coming forward. 'Let Grandma into the house, please.'

Simon plumped a cushion in the least worn armchair and patted the seat. 'I'll get the kettle on, Mum. Lunch is cooking.'

'Oh good.' Sheila beamed. 'I had a small breakfast.'

Pippa decided she might as well face it. 'Hello, Sheila.'

'Hello, Pippa.' A casual acquaintance would have found the exchange perfectly friendly, but Pippa knew she was thoroughly in the doghouse. Sheila's stiff shoulders and unsmiling eyes shouted loud and clear.

'I'll check on the joint,' said Pippa, escaping to the kitchen.

As far as she could tell in the dim light, the lamb did appear to be roasting and the potatoes were browning. She slammed the range door shut.

'Seems all right to me,' said Simon.

'Yes, but it won't be done for another hour or so. Oh God.'

'What?'

'Nothing.' A whole hour of small talk with Sheila . . .

'Very nice, dear,' said Sheila, as Simon set her tea on a small table. 'And you remembered my china cup.'

'Yes, Mum.'

'It's a lovely little cottage, isn't it,' Sheila said. 'Much bigger than it looks.'

'Still not big enough for us though, especially with number two on the way.' Pippa rubbed the bump, which was shifting a little. Must book in with the midwife.

'Oh, I don't know,' said Sheila. 'I'm sure it's cosy. Of course, your furniture is rather . . . modern.'

'Mm,' said Pippa, clamping her mouth shut.

'Anyway, we won't be here for long,' Simon said. Pippa felt his hand on her back. 'Laurel Villa awaits.'

'Indeed it does,' said Pippa, leaning into him.

The lamb was eventually dished up only half an hour later than expected, and Sheila pronounced it lovely. 'A little *pinker* than I would normally have it, but very moist. That's the beauty of a range.'

Pippa bit her tongue, and thought of the gleaming steel beast in the kitchen at Laurel Villa.

'Barbara always said my roast lamb was the best she'd tasted,' said Sheila wistfully, gazing at the green beans on her plate. 'Poor Barbara. I do hope it isn't true.'

'I imagine we shall have to wait and see,' said Simon, casting a warning eye in Freddie's direction.

'She could be sharp,' Sheila continued. 'I mean, even I felt the rough end of her tongue on one occasion. But she had a good heart.' She took a gulp from her glass of red wine and swallowed, nodding to herself.

'The butcher's good, isn't he?' Simon cut in. 'And very reasonably priced, I thought. Do you go to him, Mum?'

'Of course,' sniffed Sheila. 'Meat from a supermarket isn't the same.'

The meal progressed. Pippa and Simon batted observations and comments back and forth like a pair of professional tennis players, although every so often Sheila would lob in a curve ball of 'Barbara always said . . .'

Freddie managed half a plate of roast dinner cut up small, then played a lone game of pea football with two green beans for goalposts. 'Are you finished, Freddie?' Pippa took his plate into the kitchen.

As she scraped his leftovers into the bin, Sheila's voice rose. 'I have to say, dear, I *am* offended.' Pippa set her jaw, put the plate on the worktop and returned to the dining table.

'Who wants pudding?' said Simon, a ghastly smile spreading over his face.

'Me!' shouted Freddie.

'Oh, I'm quite full,' said Sheila. 'Don't bother on my account. I think just a little rest. Perhaps with a cup of tea.'

'I'll get the kettle on,' said Pippa. 'As I'm up.' *Oh no, dear, don't bother, I'll make it*, she sing-songed in her head. Words she couldn't imagine Sheila saying.

'I wouldn't have thought it of her. A *nasty* thing to put in a text message.'

Pippa banged mugs on the worktop.

'And so soon after, too . . .'

Pippa filled the kettle noisily at the tap, thumped it down, and switched it on.

'Maybe she's a bit . . . don't some pregnant women go a bit *funny*?'

'Mum, that's enough now.'

Pippa wrenched open the window and leaned on the worktop, taking in deep lungfuls of the damp October air. *It's a good thing I know I didn't do it*, she thought, *because there are times when I know I could murder someone. And this is one of those times.*

CHAPTER 15

'What are you doing?' Simon stared at Pippa.

'What does it look like I'm doing?' Pippa held up the wine bottle and a glass.

'Having a drink.'

'Yup.' Pippa poured herself half a glass of red wine. 'Freddie's napping, you've dropped Sheila off, and I am having a small glass of wine.' She took a sip, then another. It burned her throat a little. Mmm, she'd missed this.

'Fair enough.'

'Want one?' Pippa waved a hand at the bottle. 'We can share a glass.'

Simon shook his head regretfully. 'Best not. Work to do.' He put his laptop bag on the dining-room table and unzipped it.

'What, now? No post-mortem of that awful lunch?'

'I'd rather not, thanks.' He sat down.

'Do you have to? Can't it wait?' Pippa uncurled herself, went over, and put her arms around him from behind. Perhaps it was the wine, but she definitely felt more benevolent towards Simon than she had for some time. That could be because he'd packed Sheila off in fairly short order. As soon as she'd finished her tea (which Pippa had had to decant into the china cup), Simon had her coat ready.

Simon disengaged her, gently. 'It's a lovely offer, but I have loads to do. Presentations for next week, and a couple of reports to write. Spreadsheets and everything.'

'Can I help? I'm good at spreadsheets.'

The corners of Simon's mouth curved upwards, then fell as quickly. 'Pippa, it's fine. Why don't you get your feet up.'

Her feet would get tired of being up. Pippa settled in the armchair with a library book. Perhaps she shouldn't complain. Not the weekend she'd envisaged, though. She glanced across at the top of Simon's head, bent to his laptop, the keys clacking rapidly.

A tap at the front door startled her. Who was it? Perhaps Marge, to see if the phone had come back to life? She genuinely couldn't think of anyone else who might drop by unannounced on a Saturday afternoon.

Pippa padded to the door, and opened it cautiously.

On the step, her hand raised to tap again, stood Lila. Her hair was wild, and there were dark shadows under her eyes. 'Oh thank God, I thought you might be out, but I saw a light on. I'm sorry to barge in on you —'

'Lila, what is it?' Lila's eyes darted about, taking in Simon working at the table, the wine glass by the armchair, the book.

'I'm sorry, I've come at a bad time —'

'No, no, come in.' Pippa opened the door fully, took Lila's arm, and guided her into the house. 'You look terrible. What is it?'

'You're busy. I should go, I'm disturbing you. I

94

shouldn't have come . . .'

Pippa glanced towards Simon, whose head stayed firmly bent over his laptop. 'Simon, can you keep an ear open for Freddie for a few minutes?' Simon nodded, eyes on the screen. 'Kitchen, Lila.'

She steered Lila in and closed the door. It wasn't any more private than talking in the sitting room, but it felt like it. 'Please, what is it? Where's Bella?'

'I dropped her off at my sister's. I didn't know where to go —' Lila broke off, looking stricken. 'Have you been called in to the police station yet? God, Pippa, I'm sorry, I didn't even ask —'

'Yes, I went yesterday morning.'

'And it was OK?'

'Well, as OK as it can be —'

'They called me in yesterday afternoon. Apparently I'm a potential suspect.' Lila's voice wrung the words dry.

'But aren't we all suspects? It must have been one of us —'

'Did they caution you?'

Pippa shook her head.

'See?' Lila began to pace, a tough task in a kitchen as small as Pippa's. 'They said it was suspicious that I'd left early. They said several people had told I didn't like Barbara and made no secret of it.' Lila ran her hands through her hair. 'I was in there for — it felt like hours. They cross-examined me, the pair of them, but they were both the bad cop. They said it had been reported that I went to the toilet not long before eleven, so I had a good chance of doing it.' She dashed the back of her hand across her eyes. 'I didn't do it, but I don't think they believed me.' She came to a rest against the range, and sniffled. 'I'm

95

sorry, Pippa. I didn't mean to come and wreck your weekend.'

'But why me?' said Pippa, putting an arm round her. 'What about the others?'

'Don't you see?' wailed Lila. 'How do I know one of them didn't do it? What if I find out I'm the only suspect? What if someone lies, says they saw me go into the kitchen? I can't prove I didn't! What would happen to Bella?' She sobbed into Pippa's shoulder.

'Ssh, ssh . . .' Pippa soothed Lila automatically, just as she would have Freddie. 'But why would anyone think you'd do it? I mean, lots of people had reasons to dislike Barbara.'

'I'm expendable,' Lila said simply, wiping her eyes. 'I'm a single parent, I haven't been here long, and I'm a mouthy cow. I bet some people would love to see me go. And if they can't pin it on me, I bet they'll whisper it, until I slink off with my tail between my legs. That'll teach me for trying to give my kid a better life.' She smacked the worktop, then put her hand to her mouth. 'Shit, sorry Pippa. Oh heck, I've probably woken Freddie now. I should go.'

'No. Stay. You were the first person I spoke to in the village who was actually nice to me. And I don't believe you did it. I can imagine you shouting at Barbara. I can imagine you having a full-on row with her. But I can't imagine you sneaking up on her and whacking her on the head.' Pippa patted Lila's arm. 'You couldn't stay quiet that long.'

Lila sniffed. 'Thanks . . . I think.' Her mouth wobbled upwards a tiny bit.

'Do you have any idea who might have done it?' Pippa

asked.

Lila shook her head. 'No-one, and everyone. That's the worst. Well, none of us liked her, you know that from the conversation in the pub after — after it happened.' She pushed her hair back. 'But there was nothing bad enough to kill someone over. Just niggles. As far as I know.' She sighed. 'I keep going round in circles. I haven't told my family yet, because they'd worry. I had to make up a last-minute pedicure to get Serena to have Bella. Oh God, the police would probably say I'm a natural liar.'

'We must find out who did it,' said Pippa decisively.

'But how?' Lila spread her hands, helplessly. It was the first time Pippa had ever seen Lila look anything close to helpless.

'Through detective work, I suppose.' Pippa half-smiled. 'I'd better get on and finish the Miss Marple book I'm reading.'

Lila half-snorted, half-hiccuped. 'Aren't you a bit young for Miss Marple?'

'True,' said Pippa. 'I should model myself on the pregnant cop in *Fargo*.' She shivered. 'I hope it doesn't get as cold as North Dakota here. I'm no fan of snow.'

'But how are you going to do it?' Lila persisted. 'Not that I think you're stupid or anything, but —'

'Honestly, I don't know.' Pippa leaned against the worktop. 'But if the police really believe you did it, maybe they're a bit stupid. Unless they think you're shielding someone, and they're trying to scare you into talking.'

Lila snorted, properly this time. 'It would be interesting to find out if anyone else got the same treatment. I mean, they were properly nasty to me.'

'Do you want a drink?' asked Pippa. 'There's tea, or

coffee, or wine if you like.'

Lila shook her head. 'I'd love a glass of wine, but better not. I should go and get Bella. I said I wouldn't be long. I hope Serena doesn't ask to see my feet.' She straightened up. 'Thanks, Pippa, I — I feel a bit better.'

'Good.' Pippa gave Lila a hug. 'Try not to worry. And tell me if anything happens. What's your mobile number?'

Lila got out her phone and showed Pippa the number. Pippa typed it into her contacts. 'I'll text you and then you've got my number too.'

'Thanks,' Lila stuffed her phone in her pocket. 'You've been very kind, Pippa. I won't forget.'

'S'OK,' Pippa said.

'How long is Simon back for?' Lila asked.

'Just the weekend,' said Pippa. 'He's working now.'

'Ugh,' said Lila. 'I'll leave you to it. Give Freddie a hug from Bella.'

Pippa walked Lila to the front door. 'Shall we meet next week? What about playgroup?'

'The church hall's been taped off since it happened,' said Lila. 'The SlimFit people were furious . . . Wait,' she exclaimed. 'The playgroup in Gadding Parva meets on Tuesday afternoons. We could go. I'll text the others so it doesn't look weird, you and I going off together.'

'You make it sound like we're having an affair,' said Pippa.

'Hah,' said Lila. 'Being a bad influence yet again. Say hi to your husband, and do explain I'm not usually this odd.'

'I wouldn't worry,' said Pippa. 'He lives with me, after all.'

She shut the door gently once Lila had gone, and turned

back to Simon, whose head had lifted from the laptop screen at last. 'Sorry.'

'Was that one of your playgroup people?'

'That's right. Lila.'

'Is she usually like that?'

'Talkative, yes. Noisy, yes. Out of her mind with worry, no.' Pippa walked towards the table. Simon closed the laptop as she sat beside him. 'The police were pretty harsh with her.'

'And you're sure she didn't do it?'

'As sure as I can be.' Pippa grimaced. 'I want to believe no-one did it, or a stranger who escaped through an invisible air duct. Whatever.'

'I hope you were joking about investigating, Pippa.' Simon's face was serious. 'That's what the police are for. Don't go being a hero and getting yourself into danger.'

'Don't be daft, Simon, I can barely tie my shoelaces, never mind catch a murderer.' She sighed. 'When are you due back at work?'

'Breakfast meeting in Manchester on Monday. Seven-thirty start. Not my choice, I assure you,' he said in response to Pippa's wrinkled nose. 'I'll have to get the train up tomorrow, and I'm there all week. I'd drive it, but I'd have to start at daft o'clock in the morning. No point waking you and Freddie.'

'I s'pose. It's been nice.' Pippa reached for his hand and played with his fingers.

'You're distracting me, aren't you?'

'Might be,' said Pippa. 'Freddie's still asleep.'

As if on cue, a bellow of 'Mummy!' came from above them.

'I'll go,' said Simon. 'But first, promise me not to play

the sleuth. I don't want to open the paper over breakfast in some hotel and read that you're the next victim.'

'No, Simon,' said Pippa, as he climbed the stairs. But he definitely couldn't see her fingers crossed under the table.

CHAPTER 16

Pippa felt an unexpected pang as they waved Simon off at Gadcester station, and watched the train ease away. Freddie had insisted they go all the way to the station to say goodbye, although Pippa suspected that seeing the train might be a factor too. 'Bye-bye, Daddy!' Freddie shouted, still waving at the shrinking dot. 'Bye-bye!' Then he looked at Pippa. 'Cake?'

'What a good idea, Freddie.'

They found a cafe on the main street and Freddie chose the most lurid cake on display. Pippa, after surveying the various options, settled on shortbread. 'Mummy . . .' said Freddie, 'when are we going home?'

Pippa sipped her coffee. 'When you've finished your cake and milk, Freddie.'

'No,' Freddie's face screwed up a little, as if she had said something particularly silly. 'Real home.'

Pippa stopped mid-sip. 'Real home?'

'Yes. Park, tube.' Freddie drew a huge circle in the air. 'Big London.'

Pippa put her cup down. 'Freddie . . . we live in Much Gadding now. I know the house we're in at the moment isn't —'

'Wanna go home.' Freddie sniffed.

So do I. 'Come for a cuddle, Freddie. What do you miss?'

'Jake . . . William . . . the park . . . the sweet shop . . .' The sniffing, while muffled, grew more frequent.

'I miss home too,' said Pippa. 'But you've met Bella, and Grace, and you'll meet other people. And Much Gadding must have a sweet shop. I'm sure we'll like it just as much.'

'Yeah?' Freddie twisted round with shining eyes.

'Yeah. Now eat your cake, or I might have to pinch it.'

'Nooooo!' Freddie ran round the table and seized his cake, cramming most of it into his mouth in one go.

Could we go back to London? thought Pippa, as she drove along the winding road to Much Gadding. The flat was sold, but they could find something, maybe a doer-upper . . . they'd need a extra bedroom . . . She imagined Simon's face if she brought it up. 'But why?' he'd say. 'You've got the countryside on your doorstep, good schools, a community. Most people would kill for that.'

And someone had. Pippa shook herself and focused on the road. She'd driven the last couple of miles in a daydream.

When Freddie was in bed, Pippa hunted in the chest of drawers for a notepad. She sat at the dining table and wrote *Barbara Hamilton — Murder* at the top of the page. Then she wrote *Known facts*, underlined it twice, and stared at it.

Lots of people didn't like her. But was that true, or was it just the people she'd met? Sheila had said Barbara had a good heart.

Friends with Sheila.

Hit on the back of the head. What had PC Horsley said? A depressed cranial fracture. That sounded as if she'd been hit either very hard, or with something pretty heavy. Something heavy made sense. But what? And was it something the person — the murderer — had brought with them, or something already there? Pippa drew an arrow and wrote *Examine crime scene.* That felt official. Although she wasn't sure how to do it. *Check if church hall has reopened.* She could stroll past on a walk with Freddie tomorrow.

What else did she know about Barbara? Pippa racked her brains to remember what Lila had told her on their first meeting.

Women's Institute
Pre-school board
Primary school governor
Parish council
???

Pippa made a face. How on earth was she supposed to make sense of it? *That's why they have policemen, idiot.* She closed the pad, put it in the drawer, and grabbed her phone.

'Pip! Hi!' Suze shouted into the phone. 'I thought you'd fallen into a combine harvester!' Rock music blared in the background.

'Very funny.' Pippa walked upstairs and pushed open the bathroom door. 'Can you turn the music down?'

'I'm in the pub!'

'Oh, OK.'

'So what's going on in the back of beyond?'

'There's been a murder.' Pippa sat on the edge of the bath.

103

'Hang on, you're a bit crackly. I'll try the other ear.' Pippa winced at the clatter and whistle. 'I thought you said murder!'

'I did.'

'Oh. Oh shit. Sorry.' The rock music faded. 'I'm going outside,' yelled Suze. 'Who?'

'The woman who runs the playgroup. And I was there when it happened.'

'What, you mean you *saw* it?'

'You're still shouting, Suze.'

'Sorry,' Suze's voice went down a few notches. 'But that is pretty hardcore.'

'I didn't see it happen, it was in the kitchen. We were in the hall.'

'Woooww. Have they arrested anyone?'

'I don't think so.' Pippa shifted her weight slightly. 'But they cautioned someone I know. She's in bits.'

'Do you think she did it?'

'Of course not!'

'Well, someone must have. What did the police say?'

'It only happened on Thursday.' Pippa could scarcely believe it. Thursday seemed a world away.

'What's it called, where you live? I'll look on the web.'

'Much Gadding.' Of course! Pippa slapped herself gently on the side of the head. The internet!

'Are you all right?' Suze's voice had taken on what Pippa thought of as its mother hen quality.

'Yes. Yes fine. Well. Not really. Freddie's homesick. And so am I.'

'Well, come down next weekend. I can put you up, if you don't mind the futon.'

'I'd love to, but I'm not sure I can. The police said we

all had to stick around.'

A pause. 'Is that because you're under suspicion?' Suze's voice had a giggle underneath, waiting to escape. 'Mrs Parker, in the kitchen, with the lead piping?'

'Don't!' Pippa cried. 'That's how she died, someone bashed her head in.'

'Oh God. Sorry. Try to come down. Maybe if you give the police my details . . . tell them I'm a responsible law-abiding citizen.'

'I'll get done for perjury.'

Suze snorted. 'See, you can still laugh. Text me.'

'Will do.' The rock music was getting louder again. 'Bye, Suze.'

'Bye Pip.' A final *thump-thump-thump,* and the call ended.

Pippa went downstairs to warm up, rubbing her arms. Visiting Suze would be lovely, if PC Horsley let her go. But Simon would be at home alone. And she didn't fancy Suze's futon. And she'd have to sleep with Freddie, so neither of them would sleep. And what if she went into labour? Oh God, what if her waters broke *on the futon*? She'd never hear the end of it. Get a grip, Pippa.

She attempted an internet search for Much Gadding on her phone, but found only a sad-faced cloud. Huh. At least the broadband installation was already booked for Laurel Villa. But somewhere in the village would have a wi-fi hotspot. Surely. Pippa lowered herself into the armchair and opened *The Body in the Library*. She'd learn from the experts. Plus, if she asked PC Horsley about visiting Suze, she could ask how the case was progressing . . . hmm . . . Now what questions should she ask? Pippa fell into a pleasant haze where she would pump PC Horsley for information, gently but skilfully, and unmask the murderer, pointing an accusing finger. 'You!'

She woke with a start, blinking at the bright light from the lampshade overhead. Miss Marple never fell asleep on the job. Pippa had lost her place in the book, too. She flicked through the pages, looking for the last bit she remembered. But she had read it so many times that it all seemed familiar. 'I give up,' she said aloud.

Her watch said half-past nine. Maybe a cup of tea would help, and stuff the caffeine. She flicked the kettle on and reached for the jar of teabags. Next to it was the jar of rice. She took it down, and reached in for the phone Freddie had rescued. It still wouldn't switch on. She wiped some mud off the screen with her thumb. It wasn't a smartphone, just an ordinary mobile with a plain, champagne-coloured case. But how had it got into the river?

The kettle pinged. Pippa put the phone on the worktop and reached for the teabags. She poured hot water into her Buffy mug, and studied the phone. It was an old model, but in good condition; no scratches, and screen intact. The sort of phone you might give your mum or gran, for emergencies, and which you knew she'd probably never use the credit on. But why would a phone like that end up in the river? It would be tucked away safely. It might not even leave the house . . .

You're going doolally, Pippa Parker. It's a phone. She put it back into the rice, and replaced the jar on the shelf. *And the only way you'll learn anything about it is if you can get it working again.* She finished making her tea, and settled in the armchair with her book, opening it at random. That made as much sense as anything else.

CHAPTER 17

Pippa was up early the next day, so much so that Freddie had to be gently, then less gently, persuaded awake. 'Come on Freddie, breakfast time!'

'It's dark,' moaned Freddie. 'I can't seeeeeee . . .'

Pippa snapped the light on. 'There you go.'

Having urged Freddie through his toast, wash, teeth, and getting dressed, Pippa was ready to leave the house when she remembered the thing about Mondays. Nothing was open. Except the pub. And that wouldn't be open yet. Or maybe she hadn't looked hard enough last week. Anyway. 'Let's go and feed the ducks!' she sang, diving into the kitchen and emerging with a couple of slices of bread in her hand.

Freddie jumped along beside her, his earlier sleepiness forgotten. 'We could walk around the village first,' said Pippa. 'Would you like that?'

'Ducks!' protested Freddie. 'Hungry ducks!'

The duck pond in the middle of the three-cornered village green reflected the blue of the sky, and birds were singing in the trees. It was quite nice really. Pippa handed Freddie a slice of bread. A glossy-headed mallard swam

107

over and waddled towards them.

'Oi!' shouted a crumpled old man sitting on the bench nearby. 'You shouldn't feed 'em bread! They want duck food!' Freddie was already throwing bread at the duck, which bent and gobbled it. Another piece hit the duck on the head, but it didn't seem bothered.

Pippa turned to the old man. 'All right, where sells duck food?'

He pointed with his stick. 'Country store.' A light shone in the window. 'You'd better get a move on, they shut in a minute. They're only open Monday for the papers.'

'Thanks,' Pippa grabbed Freddie's hand. 'Come on Freddie, we'll get duck food.' Freddie dropped the rest of his bread on the floor and the duck gulped it down.

They ran across the green and reached the shop as the lights went off. 'Darn!' Pippa pushed the door, which, to her surprise, opened. A bell rang inside the shop.

'Er, hello?' The inside of the shop was surprisingly dark. It smelt of sawdust and, a bit, of wet dog. 'Hello?'

'Yes, what is it?' A small wiry man in a pale brown coat appeared from the back room.

'Do you have any . . . any duck food?' Pippa asked, feeling thoroughly ridiculous.

'We do!' The man retrieved a small bag of something with a strong resemblance to sawdust from under the counter. 'Fifty pee. Anything else?'

'Erm, I don't think so . . .' Pippa pulled out her purse and walked up to the counter. 'Oh!'

'Look, Mummy!' cried Freddie. 'Play lady!'

'Yes.' Pippa stared at the newspaper on top of the pile. A large photo of Barbara occupied the middle of the front page, underneath the headline 'LOCAL WOMAN

MURDERED'.

'Are you planning to buy a copy?' said the man, mildly. 'The library's where you read for free.'

'Oh yes. Of course. Sorry.' Pippa picked up the paper and folded it in half.

'One pound ten.' She fumbled in her purse and handed him the right money.

'What about sweets?' said Freddie, pointing at the bags of humbugs swinging from a stand on the counter. 'You said we'd find a sweet shop.'

'All right.' Pippa unhooked a bag and put it on the paper.

'Anything else?' said the man. 'Butterfly net, pair of waders, kitchen sink?'

'No, thank you.' Pippa said firmly.

'Good. Two sixty, please.' Pippa added a two pound coin to the money in the man's hand. He frowned at it, put his finger on a fifty pence piece from the row of coins on the counter, and slid it towards her.

'Thank you,' said Pippa, backing away. 'Bye.'

'Bye!' shouted Freddie, as the bell jangled. The man, watching them, turned the sign to 'Closed'. She handed the bag of duck food to Freddie.

'Sweet!'

'You've just had breakfast, Freddie. All right, one.' She put the paper under her arm and opened the packet. She fancied a sweet herself. 'Now, I'm going to sit on this bench. Don't go too near the water.'

Freddie stood ten feet from the pond, lobbing handfuls of flakes at the ducks. Pippa looked at the photo of Barbara. She wore a smart floral dress with a pale blue blazer and a pillbox hat, and she had a wide, frozen smile on her face.

'Much Gadding resident Barbara Hamilton was found murdered on Thursday morning at St Saviour's church hall. It is understood that a playgroup session was taking place at the time.

Mrs Hamilton was a well-known member of the community who had given her time unsparingly to public service since moving into the village, following the death of her husband. She was president of the WI, a parish councillor, and served on various local committees. Mrs Sheila Parker, a fellow Much Gadding resident and a close friend of Mrs Hamilton, said "I'm absolutely devastated. I can't understand why anyone would murder Barbara. It makes me wonder if any of us are safe in our beds." A full obituary of Mrs Hamilton can be found on page 28.

Inspector Fanshawe of Gadcestershire Police, who is in charge of the investigation, assured our reporter that several lines of enquiry are open, and they are confident of making progress on the case. Any members of the public who feel they have information relevant to the case are encouraged to contact PC Horsley at Much Gadding police station (839426) as soon as possible.'

Pippa looked up from the page. Freddie shook the last scraps from the bag of duck food, watched by the old man on the next bench. She folded the paper with the back page outermost, and got to her feet.

'Terrible business, ain't it,' remarked the old man, still watching Freddie.

'I'm sorry?'

'The murder.' The man coughed. 'She crossed a lot of people, but she did a lot of good, too. This place won't be the same without her.'

'Did you know her well?' Pippa allowed herself to linger by the bench.

'Not well as such, but I go to the Wednesday lunch club at the church hall. She directed operations, so to speak. There was nothing like that before she came. She shook things up properly, did Barbara Hamilton. I hope someone will take it on, or it will all go back the way it was. Second-home folk down at the weekends, and the village like a ghost town. Oh you may smile, young lady, but those hanging baskets, and the fancy signs, and the benches, they didn't get here by themselves. Someone's got to do it, and whatever her faults, Barbara was a doer.' He nodded, emphatically. 'There. I've said my bit, and I hope they find whoever did it and give 'em what for.' He smacked his fist into his palm.

'Er, yes, I hope they do too.' Pippa edged away from the bench. 'Freddie!' Freddie was deep in conversation with a duck. 'Do you want another sweet?' He came running.

'You'll rot his teeth, you know,' said the old man, grimly.

'An occasional treat is fine,' said Pippa, and walked off as the old man said something about rationing.

She unwrapped the promised sweet and popped it into Freddie's mouth, then took his hand. 'Time for our walk.'

Over the road, past Polly's Whatnots (closed), and into the conservation area. Past St Saviour's —

'Where we going, Mummy?' asked Freddie. 'Playgroup?'

'No, Freddie, it isn't on today.' Pippa quickened her pace and peered through the trees. No lights, but no police tape either. She gasped and jumped back as the door of the

111

church hall opened and PC Horsley came out.

'Ow!' cried Freddie. 'You hurt my arm, Mummy!'

'What's that?' called PC Horsley. 'Is someone there?'

Swearing fluently to herself, Pippa stepped onto the path. 'I was walking past. You startled me.'

PC Horsley closed the door and locked it, then walked towards her, taking his time. 'Did I.' His eyes were hidden under the peak of his cap. 'Why would that be?' He glanced at the paper tucked under her arm.

'I'm a bit jumpy.' *Shut up, Pippa.*

'Yes. I suppose you would be.' He looked down his nose at her, and adjusted his hat. 'Any particular reason why you're walking by the church hall?'

Pippa remembered the old man's words. *Someone's got to do it.* 'Can we still use it? For the playgroup, I mean. We should still run it, shouldn't we? It's a community resource.'

'It is.' PC Horsley locked eyes with Pippa. 'I don't see why not. We finished here on Friday. Not that there was much.'

'Did you find anything?' Pippa tried to keep her voice casual.

'Well, we don't know whodunnit, if that's what you mean. Found the weapon, though. That little fire extinguisher hung up by the kitchen door. Matched exactly. Makes things quite interesting.'

'How do you mean?'

'It only weighs a couple of kilos. So it wouldn't take a circus strongman to give it a good swing.' PC Horsley's eyes didn't move from Pippa's face. 'I'll get you a key cut for the door.' His mouth twitched. 'So you can run your playgroup. I'll ring you when it's ready.'

'What? Oh yes. Thank you.'

PC Horsley stood on the path, and Pippa gathered she was dismissed. She walked back towards River Lane, feeling slightly battered.

'Mummy . . .' Freddie tugged her sleeve. 'Is there a circus?'

'No, no circus, Freddie.' Pippa thought it over. 'Well, not that kind of circus, anyway.'

CHAPTER 18

'So what's it like?' Pippa asked, as Lila's Fiat pootled along the road to Gadding Parva. Freddie and Bella were singing along to the radio, or, more accurately, making noises at the same time.

'The playgroup?' Lila's eyes flicked across. 'Not that different from Gadding Goslings. Except their woman in charge isn't a dragon like Barbara — was.' Her hands tightened on the wheel. 'I don't think I'll ever get used to that. She was such a character. Like a pantomime villain. We all loved to hate her.' She bit her lip. 'That sounds awful, doesn't it? But she played up to it. Or maybe we just told ourselves that.'

'Maybe,' said Pippa. The road took a sharp bend to the right, and a pocket-sized village swung into view. A green, a church, a row of cottages. 'Wow, it's even smaller than Much Gadding.'

'Yeah, this is the model village version. Here we are.' Lila indicated and pulled into a small piece of waste ground in front of a wooden chalet. 'Parva Pandas.' Several cars were parked already. 'Nick's here. And Caitlin.' She switched the radio off. 'Stop caterwauling,

114

you two.'

A buzz emanated from the chalet. Pippa hung back a little in the porch, and Lila looked at her questioningly. 'Go on,' said Pippa, taking a deep breath.

As on her first visit to Gadding Goslings, all eyes turned to them, and Pippa was doubly glad that she and Lila had come together. Nick waved from where he knelt on the floor, playing a game with Grace. Sam and Caitlin were talking, holding mugs out of the children's reach. Most of the people, whom Pippa didn't recognise, glanced at her for a second or two before resuming their conversations. A long-haired woman in a beaded top and tie-dye skirt unfolded herself from the floor and strolled towards them.

'Hello, Lila,' she said, encircling her in an airy embrace. 'Welcome to Parva Pandas,' she said to Pippa, performing a slightly remoter version of the same. 'My name is Marina. Come and sit down.' She descended gracefully into the lotus position.

Freddie and Bella had already wandered over to Grace. Nearby, Henry played with his steering wheel in great contentment.

'Do you mind if I take a chair?' she said to Marina. 'I'm not sure I'll get up again if I sit on the floor.'

'If you think so,' said Marina. 'I find the floor much more comfortable. But I've always been flexible.'

Lila fetched two chairs for them, winking at Pippa as she took her seat.

'Well, there isn't much to say about the playgroup, really.' Marina gazed at the children and parents. 'It sort of runs itself. Tea and coffee facilities are on the table — decaf, camomile, peppermint — and biscuits in the tin. Just pay for what you have. We all pitch in to unpack and put

115

away . . . yes, it is a harmonious group.' She seemed about to go into a trance; then her eyes snapped open. 'I must refill the biscuits.' She rose to her feet. 'They're vegan and gluten-free, so you don't have to worry. I make them myself.' She rummaged in a hessian bag placed under the table, extracted a plastic container, and transferred greyish bars to the tin.

Nick waggled his eyebrows from his seat on the floor. Grace had tired of the game and was playing with a tiny blonde-haired girl. Pippa smiled at him. Nick got a chair and joined them. 'So we're all still at large,' he observed.

'Apparently so,' said Lila. 'Even me.'

'Don't be daft, Lila,' said Nick. 'There's no reason for them to suspect you more than anyone else.'

'Tell them that.' Lila folded her arms and stared at the wall.

'I think we should start the playgroup back up,' said Pippa.

Nick and Lila looked at her, eyebrows raised. 'Would people come?' said Nick, slowly. 'It's very soon after . . .' He scratched his nose. 'And the playgroup was Barbara's thing.'

'Yes, and maybe it shouldn't have been.' Pippa leaned forward as far as her bump would permit. 'This is our chance to shape the playgroup so it's the way we would like it to be.'

'You're right,' said Lila. 'A group of us could do it. Come on, Nick.'

Nick studied the floor. 'It's a bit too soon for me. Maybe in the future, but not right now.' He watched Grace playing with her new friend. 'I think it's got to me a bit more than I realised.'

'Fair enough,' said Lila. 'Let us know when you're ready. And we can still come here.'

'Yeah,' said Nick, absently. 'Thanks for texting me about today. Good that we're all sticking together.'

'I'm going to recruit Sam and Caitlin,' said Lila, standing up. 'And get a brew, too. Anyone else?'

'If anything's got caffeine in it, yes,' said Pippa. Lila went to inspect the table and shook her head glumly before wandering towards their fellow playgroup members, who were watching their children play.

'Have you been for your police interview yet?' Pippa jumped at Nick's question. Her mind had been drifting on the subject of the wonderful new playgroup of opportunity.

'Yes, I went on Friday. You?'

'Yeah. Same. I suspect they got us all in that day.' He leaned towards Pippa, and she caught a faint whiff of his aftershave. 'I don't see how they're going to solve it. Too many people, with no proper motive.'

'No,' said Pippa. She had forgotten how dark Nick's eyes were. Like rich dark chocolate . . .

'Er, excuse me?' The speaker was a short dark-haired woman in jeans, with a toddler on her hip. 'I hope you don't mind me asking, but . . . are you from the Much Gadding playgroup? Where *it* happened?' Her eyes were round, showing the whites.

'Yes, we are,' said Pippa.

'Ooh,' said the woman. 'That must have been weird.'

'Yes. It was,' said Pippa. 'Nick, I might get a brew —'

'Did you see anything?' The toddler pulled at the woman's hair, and she put his hand aside.

'No,' said Nick.

The woman looked at Pippa.

'No,' said Pippa.

'And the Inspector from Gadcester is involved, isn't he?'

'I believe so,' said Pippa, getting to her feet.

'I'll get you a brew, Pippa,' Nick got up too.

'I might have a biscuit . . . Excuse me,' she said to the woman. Pippa peeked from the refreshment table, and she still stood by their chairs, waiting to resume her interrogation.

The grey biscuits were no pleasanter on a close inspection. 'I miss cake,' said Pippa. 'What happened to the cake I brought last Thursday? I'd completely forgotten it till now. It wasn't much of a loss, mind you.'

'It's probably Exhibit A.' Nick nudged her, gently. 'I imagine the policemen commandeered it. It'll be long eaten.'

'I might ask PC Horsley,' said Pippa.

'How was your weekend?' asked Nick. 'Did your husband get down?'

'Yes. Although he invited his mother for lunch on Saturday, and he had to go back on Sunday afternoon.'

'Oh. There are chairs free next to Lila.' Nick pointed, and as Pippa looked, he bent to her ear. 'I'd have thought he would want to spend time with you. And Freddie, of course.'

'His mum was friends with Barbara,' said Pippa. 'She's had a big shock.'

'Mm,' said Nick. 'And you haven't, of course.' And he walked towards the chairs, leaving Pippa to follow.

Pippa stared after him. Nick took the chair beside Lila and began talking. She took her time in joining them.

'Are you all right, Pippa?' asked Sam. 'You seemed a

bit . . . well, lost.'

'Yes, I'm fine,' Pippa said automatically. 'So should we restart the playgroup?'

'Yeah, definitely,' said Caitlin. 'But someone has to be in charge.' She looked at Pippa.

'Yes, as a contact,' said Sam. 'It probably isn't much work.' She, too, looked at Pippa.

'Don't both rush at once,' said Pippa.

'It isn't that,' said Caitlin. 'I'm returning to work next month, and I don't know my hours yet.'

Sam chimed in. 'And I've got —'

'OK, whatever. I don't mind. PC Horsley's getting a key cut for me, anyway. So I guess I'm it by default. But do you think people will come? After —'

'Oh God, yes,' said Lila. 'We might have to go to the loo in threes, though. And lock away the kitchen knives.'

'That isn't funny,' said Nick shortly. 'Anyway, I'd better be off. I have a conference call in half an hour.' Pippa watched his tall form stalk towards Marina, who was reading a story to a ring of children, and then stride off.

'Nick's rattled,' said Lila. 'Wonder why?'

'Maybe he's worried people will point the finger at him,' said Caitlin. 'After all, he was the only man there. He could easily have taken a swing at Barbara.'

'Any of us could.' Pippa leaned in close and told the group what PC Horsley had said about the fire extinguisher.

'Ooo,' said Sam, wrinkling her nose.

'Anyway, it's settled,' said Lila. 'Pippa's in charge. Can we be ready by Thursday?'

'Yes, if I have a key. I'll text round, either way. Will you come and help me set up?'

They all nodded agreement. 'To Gadding Goslings!' Caitlin raised her mug of green tea.

'To Gadding Goslings,' they echoed.

CHAPTER 19

Pippa's phone rang as Lila started the car to drive them back from Parva Pandas. The display said *Police*. 'Hello?'

'Is that Mrs Parker?' She recognised PC Horsley's voice.

'It is, yes.'

'This is Police Constable Horsley.' He paused, at which Pippa itched to say *Yes, I know*. 'You can come and get your key tomorrow.'

'Oh. Thanks.'

'Ten o'clock all right?'

'Yes, perfect.' Well, it would get her out of bed, anyway.

'Right. Goodbye, Mrs Parker.' The phone went dead.

'Hot date?' asked Lila, changing gear.

'Hardly,' Pippa smiled. 'PC Horsley, to say the key for the church hall is ready.'

'Oh, right.' Lila stopped to let a woman with a buggy cross the road. 'That's weird.'

'Is it?'

'Well, wouldn't the caretaker do that?'

'I suppose . . .' Pippa watched the road for a bit. 'What

do you think?'

'I don't know.' Lila voice was light. Too light. 'Maybe he's monitoring who has keys to the hall.'

'But why would it matter now?'

'Dunno. Here we are.' Lila pulled up at the mouth of River Lane. 'Can you manage?'

'Yeah.' Pippa got herself and Freddie out of the car, and reached in for his car seat. 'See you on Thursday, Lila.'

'Yup. Bye!' The Fiat did a neat three-point turn, and accelerated away.

Pippa stood looking after the rapidly diminishing car. Freddie pulled at her arm. 'Snack, Mummy.'

Pippa sighed. 'All right, Freddie.'

'*Bad* biscuits.' Freddie stumped down the path beside her.

'Yes, naughty biscuits,' Pippa said, absently.

'Mummy!' Freddie giggled. 'Not naughty!'

'No . . . Just bad.'

'Yes. Good biscuit?' He put his head on one side.

'Yes, Freddie.' A good biscuit, or two, was an excellent idea. Pippa switched the TV on to cartoons for Freddie, and went to the kitchen. A beaker of milk and two Jammie Dodgers for him. 'Just making myself a cup of tea, Freddie.'

'OK, Mummy,' Freddie said, hugging the cushion to his chest.

Pippa checked her phone. 12% charge left. *Phew.* She plugged it into the charger. It would be her luck to let it die just before her waters broke. *I'm much more responsible than that*, she thought, leaning against the range. She scanned the shelves, waiting for the kettle to boil. It was taking its time . . . That was because she hadn't switched it

122

on! She leapt forward and flicked the switch.

And speaking of switching things on . . . She reached for the jar of rice and extracted the phone. Her thumb hovered, and she pressed the on button, once.

Nothing.

Pippa pressed it again, and held it down.

The phone lit up and she nearly dropped it.

The mystery was about to be solved! Pippa pressed *Menu*. Then *Phone Book*. Surely there would be a number for 'Home' or 'Me' or 'In Case of Emergency'. She scrolled. Lots of women's names — 'Doreen', 'Margaret', 'Sheila' — another Sheila! — 'Shirley'. Pippa rechecked the list, reading more carefully, but nothing rang a bell. Perhaps she should hand it in at the police station.

Wait. Most phones had their own number listed somewhere. Pippa went back to the menu and tried each heading. At last, under *Properties*, she found it. 07871 . . .

Where had she seen a phone number starting like that? Pippa unlocked her own phone and scrolled through her contacts. Caitlin . . . no. Lila . . . no. Nick . . . yes, but the rest of the number was wrong.

She froze. It was staring her in the face.

The number she had typed into her phone the week before, standing in front of the parish noticeboard.

Playgroup.

It was Barbara's phone.

Pippa fumbled both handsets onto the worktop. She switched the kettle on again.

I've got Barbara's phone.

Someone threw it in the river.

The murderer threw it in the river.

Freddie found it near our house.

It's got my fingerprints all over it.

She ran to the sink, retching, but nothing came out. She pushed her hair from her clammy forehead, panting.

The kettle pinged and she poured water into her cup. Too much. It spilled over and ran towards the phones. 'Shit!' She grabbed a tea towel from the oven door and mopped at the water. Then she picked up her phone and pressed *Police*.

Come on, come on . . . She shifted from one foot to the other, the phone pressed to her ear, still attached to its charging cable. The ring was like an old-fashioned phone.

'Hello,' said PC Horsley.

'Hello!' gabbled Pippa.

'You have reached Much Gadding Police Station. Unfortunately no-one is here to take your call. Please leave a message after the tone, or if your call is urgent please ring either the main switchboard at Gadcester Police Station, or dial 999. Thank you.'

Pippa rang off and glanced at the display. 4:45.

'Mummy, what are you doing?' Freddie whined from the sitting room. 'Come and watch SuperMouse!'

'All right, Freddie!' Pippa put the phone back into the jar of rice and replaced it on the shelf. She stuck a spoon into the mug of tea, realised she'd made herself a mug of now-lukewarm hot water, and poured it down the sink. She would do nothing about the phone until tomorrow. Not with Simon away. She'd probably end up having to go to Gadcester, and make a statement, and be interrogated, and probably read her rights, and . . . no.

Pippa, on autopilot, watched cartoons with Freddie, made cheesy pasta for them both, read him a bedtime story and got him settled. Her mind was on the jar of rice

124

downstairs. She tugged the kitchen blind fully down, then retrieved the phone. She pressed *Menu. Call Register. Dialled Numbers*. What date had it been? The 13th. The phone showed one call, made at 10:25, to Shelley. *Duration: 13 minutes 8 seconds.*

Pippa swore under her breath and got her notepad from the drawer. She scribbled a note, and added Shelley's phone number. As she had thought, the phone was rarely used. The previous call had been on the 11th, to Sheila. Pippa checked the number. *Our Sheila. My mother-in-law.* She wanted to cry. Instead she put the phone into the jar, and sat at the dining-room table with the notepad.

Barbara had been alive at 10.25am that morning.

Unless the murderer had done it beforehand and phoned Shelley as a red herring.

Who was Shelley? Did she have anything to do with it?

Perhaps the police could get a transcript of the call, or something?

Or was that only if they'd bugged your phone?

Oh, heck.

Pippa sat looking at the notepad for several minutes before putting it away. *You're in over your head, Pippa Parker.* She took a few deep breaths, then fetched her phone, and rang Simon.

'I can't stay on long, Pippa,' Simon's voice crackled. 'We're about to close the session.'

'Hello would be nice.' Pippa said, leaning back in her chair. It was odd how lately she always seemed to default into fighting mode when talking to Simon.

'You sound funny. What's up?'

'I . . .' She couldn't do it. She thought of the police monitoring her phone. 'I'm going to run the local playgroup.'

'You what?' Simon's voice was incredulous through the hissing.

'I'm running the playgroup.' Pippa glanced at the closed drawer where the notepad lurked. 'It won't be much work.'

'I think you'll find it's more than you bargained for,' said Simon, darkly. 'There'll be equipment, and accounts, and all sorts. There always is, with that sort of thing.'

'How would you know? You never help with stuff like that.'

'I work full time.' A lift pinged. 'You're having a baby in a few weeks, Pippa, for goodness sake. Have you registered with the doctor yet?'

'I'm going tomorrow morning,' Pippa said.

'You are now. I bet you'd forgotten. Honestly, Pippa, keep your mind on the important stuff, will you? I can't believe you phoned me at work to talk about a playgroup. Yes, I'm coming!' Simon called, 'So you'll close the deal on that. Bye now!'

Pippa quailed at the thought of the paperwork she would have to fill in at the doctor's. Simon was right, though; she should go. Even though her pregnancy was textbook, so far. She went to her changing bag and checked her maternity notes were still inside. Yes. Definitely tomorrow morning. She'd collect the church hall key afterwards. And hand in the phone. She'd probably have a better idea of what she should say to PC Horsley in the morning. She shivered a little, and checked the rice jar one more time before going upstairs.

CHAPTER 20

'Three weeks?' Pippa clutched the counter for support and stared at the receptionist.

'Well if it was up to me it'd be a lot quicker. But it isn't. The registration form has to go to the practice manager for checking, and she's on holiday in Corfu at the moment — wish I was, I've heard it's lovely at this time of year. We've had some right how-dos, you see, people getting themselves onto our list who weren't living in Gadcestershire at all! They were in the next county along! But once your registration's been processed and you've got an appointment with one of the doctors, we can refer you for midwifery care.'

'Don't you think it might be a bit late by then?' Pippa pointed at her bump.

'It's the system, that's all I can say.' The receptionist glanced past Pippa to the shuffling, muttering queue forming behind her.

'Could I register as a temporary patient?'

'Oh yes. Just fill in this form, dear. Block capitals, please.' The receptionist reached under the counter and passed a pale blue sheet to Pippa, who dutifully copied most of what she had written on the previous form. Five minutes later Pippa's and Freddie's details were in the system. 'There we are, ready to go.'

'Brilliant! Can I make an appointment, please?'

'Of course.' The receptionist peered at the screen. 'Is it an emergency?'

Pippa seethed. 'Not yet.'

'In the case, the first appointment I have is on Monday week, with Dr Paisley, at 9.20. Is that all right?'

'It'll have to be,' said Pippa.

The receptionist wrote the details on a little card and handed it to her. 'Don't forget to bring your maternity notes. Mind how you go, now.' The queue shuffled to give Pippa room, all eyeing her bump.

'Well, that's done, anyway,' Pippa said, half to herself and half to Freddie. 'Now for the police station.'

It was a beautiful autumn day, and Much Gadding looked its best. The leaves were a riot of colour, whether clinging to the trees or forming a bright splashy abstract at their feet. Freddie kicked at the carpet of leaves, which rustled up in clouds. Pippa wished they could stay and play. She glanced at St Saviour's church, austere and sharp-edged in the bright sunshine. But by the church was the little police station, and she had a job to do.

Two jobs.

'Come on, Freddie, we're popping into the police station.'

'Do we have to?' Freddie moaned.

'Yes, if you want playgroup to keep going.'

'But . . . no play lady.' Somehow, Freddie had managed to learn that the 'play lady' had gone and wasn't coming back. She assumed he must have got it from Bella or

Grace. He seemed OK about it, anyway.

'We'll have to manage by ourselves, Fred-Fred. So we need the key.' Pippa led him away from the leaves, but her steps got slower and slower as they neared the little concrete cube.

'Come on Mummy!' Freddie ran down the path and barged the door open.

'Hello, young man,' came PC Horsley's voice from inside.

'Hello policeman!' shouted Freddie.

Pippa swore under her breath and quickened her pace to her current top speed. 'Freddie, wait for me!' Once she was inside Pippa had to lean on the counter for a few seconds to catch her breath.

'Is this young man giving you the runaround, Mrs Parker?' PC Horsley's voice sounded a little stern, but under his cap he was smiling. Freddie ran to Pippa and clung to her leg.

'He's fine,' said Pippa.

'I've got your key in the office —'

'No, wait — there's something else.'

The policeman spread his hands wide on the counter. 'What kind of something else?'

'A very odd kind. Could I come into the back room? It — well — I wouldn't want someone to walk in while I tell you.'

PC Horsley's eyebrows had disappeared under his hat. Without speaking, he went to the door of the police station and drew the bolt across. Then he lifted the counter flap. 'You'd better come through. And we'd better find something for you to do, young man.' He settled Freddie in the corner with some crayons and police car pictures to colour in, and took a seat opposite Pippa. 'So what is it, Mrs Parker? Something you've forgotten to tell me? A small but vital detail?'

Pippa reached into her bag and held up the freezer bag she'd put the phone in. 'Freddie found this in the river near my house a few days ago.'

'The usual procedure is to put a notice on the parish board, Mrs Parker.' PC Horsley stretched out a hand to take the bag, but Pippa jerked it away.

'You don't understand . . . I put it in rice, to dry it —'

'Very public-spirited of you —'

'And it switched on last night —'

'Wonderful, now if you'll just —'

'And I think it's Barbara Hamilton's phone.'

PC Horsley's hand froze in mid-air. His eyes travelled slowly from the dangling phone to Pippa. 'You've got Barbara Hamilton's phone? How do you know —'

'I was trying to work out who it might belong to, so I found the phone's number. And it's the same as the one in my phone for the playgroup.'

PC Horsley snatched the bag, opened it, and looked inside. 'You do realise your fingerprints will be all over this.'

'And Freddie's, and probably Marge's — Mrs Margison, I mean,' Pippa gabbled. She took a deep breath. 'I'm guessing whoever threw it in the river gave it a good wipe first.' She clasped her shaking hands in her lap.

PC Horsley put the bag on the desk. 'Well,' he said. 'Well.' His gaze was steady, and not particularly friendly. 'And did you check anything else on the phone? We'll probably be able to track it, so you may as well tell me.'

Pippa swallowed. 'I looked at the call register. Barbara

rang someone called Shelley at 10.25 that day, and the call lasted for thirteen minutes.'

PC Horsley drew a notepad towards him and scribbled on the top sheet. He stared at his note for some seconds. 'Hmm.' He closed the notepad and put it in the desk drawer. 'It could be a coincidence.'

'Or not,' Pippa said. 'Maybe Barbara was on the phone; and if she was talking, she probably wouldn't have heard someone sneaking up on her.' She paused, then asked casually, 'Do you know who Shelley is?'

'We'll be finding out,' said PC Horsley, grimly. 'Along with sending this to be analysed.' He put the phone in the drawer with the notepad. 'Anything else? I have a few calls to make.' Freddie was colouring, his tongue stuck half-out in concentration. 'How are you getting on, Freddie?'

Freddie shouted 'Nee-naw-nee-naw!' and beamed. His police car was a cloud of blue, yellow and green scribbles. On top, a blue circle with rays of blue light coming from it. Beside the car, a stick policeman held on to a stick person wearing handcuffs.

'Exactly,' said PC Horsley. 'Very true to life, young man. I shall put it in our gallery.' Freddie gave him the picture and he studied it more closely. 'I'm checking it for clues,' he confided to Freddie.

'How's it going?' said Pippa, standing with the aid of the desk.

PC Horsley looked up from Freddie's picture, and sighed. 'It's hard going, frankly. I don't know the area, or the people. Somewhere like this, closed in on itself . . . it's difficult to get people to talk. Specially when it's a —' he glanced at Freddie, and mouthed 'murder.' He rubbed his nose. 'We're going to have to pull in friends and neighbours, because right now working on this case is like climbing a buttered cliff. Anyway.' He walked to the door and held it open. 'Let's hope your discovery moves things on. And thank you for taking the trouble. Most people would have chucked the phone back in the river, or traded it in for a fiver.' For the first time he looked at Pippa as if he didn't disapprove of her. 'We'll probably call you in to make a formal statement. Certainly if it does turn out to be Mrs Hamilton's phone.'

'OK.' Pippa slung her bag over her shoulder. It felt pounds lighter without the phone in it. 'And thank you, too, for not arresting me.'

'Pleasure,' said PC Horsley. He followed Pippa into the reception and unbolted the door. 'If you get any brainwaves, drop by.'

Pippa smiled. 'I doubt it. I can just about get through the day at the moment.' She glanced at her bump.

'Goodbye, Freddie.' PC Horsley leaned down and extended a large hand to Freddie, who pumped it as if sweets would pour from the policeman's armpit.

Pippa was almost at the street when a bellow halted her. 'Mrs Parker!' PC Horsley held up a large key. 'You forgot this.'

'Will you run and get it for me, Freddie?'

Freddie charged towards the policeman, who put the key solemnly into his palm, then ran to Pippa, bearing it like the Olympic torch.

'Thank you, Freddie.' Pippa waved to the policeman, and got her keys from her bag. 'I'll put it on here so I don't lose it.' She prised one of the rings open, wrecking her thumbnail in the process, and worked the key round. 'There.' She dropped the keys into her bag and gave a hand

132

to Freddie. As she looked up she glimpsed a woman with a buggy watching her. One of the mums from playgroup? Pippa raised a hand, but the woman was already hurrying off. *Maybe she thought I was someone else.* Pippa swung Freddie's hand. But try as she might, she couldn't swing away the feeling of someone watching her. Someone who didn't want to stop and say hello.

CHAPTER 21

Pippa exhaled cautiously as the children played in a huddle on the floor. It was going much better than she had thought it would. So far.

She had texted all the parents she knew to tell them that playgroup was restarting, and had received lots of *Great news* and *Thanks hun x* texts in reply. As promised, Lila, Sam and Caitlin had been ready and waiting when Pippa arrived at St Saviour's Church Hall at 9.45am sharp, and they had rolled their sleeves up and got stuck in. Even the little ones had helped, although they did get in everyone's way. And carry toys back to the cupboard instead of bringing more. And hide in the cupboard and jump out shouting *Boo* . . . But anyway, the playgroup was running again, she'd remembered to bring the essential supplies of tea, coffee, milk, sugar and biscuits, and Nick, lovely Nick, had brought a home-made cake.

He'd put his head round the door a few minutes before ten. 'Pippa?'

Pippa put down the chair she was carrying and waddled over. 'I thought you weren't coming!'

'I wasn't going to.' Nick opened the door and led Grace

in. 'But Henry told Grace at pre-school that the playgroup was back on, and she wanted to come.' He let go of Grace's hand and she ran straight to the toy cupboard. 'Here.' He put a canvas bag into Pippa's hand.

Pippa parted the handles. Inside the plastic box she saw the faint outline of a cake, with sweets on top. 'Oh wow! How lovely! Thanks, Nick!' On impulse she gave him a one-armed hug. His body was warm under the thin T-shirt. Pippa took her hand away hurriedly, as if it might burn.

Nick smiled at her, 'I was going to drop it off, and then I thought, how daft, and Grace would miss out, so . . .' He gave Pippa a gentle squeeze. 'So I came.'

Pippa wondered if her face was as bright a shade of red as it felt. 'I'll go and put this in the kitchen, for later.' She fanned herself once the door to the main hall was closed behind her.

Her hand trembled a little as it touched the kitchen door. *Don't be silly, Pippa*. She took a deep breath and pushed the door open, then found the little wedge and propped the door as wide as it would go. The cake was on the worktop; the urn was switched on. There. She'd gone into the kitchen, and it was fine. But she skirted round the section of floor where they had found Barbara, and her eyes avoided the fire extinguisher hanging by the door. She was glad to re-enter the main hall and sit down.

'Are you all right?' Caitlin peered into her face. 'You look like you've seen a ghost.'

Pippa tried to smile. 'Not quite. I've just been in the kitchen.'

'Oh!' Caitlin gasped and put a hand to her mouth. 'I hadn't thought . . . You should have said,' she scolded. 'One of us would have gone with you.'

135

'I didn't think,' said Pippa. 'I've wedged the kitchen door open, anyway.'

And now things seemed much as usual. Pippa had made a point of chatting to as many people as she could, and everyone said they were glad the group was running again, and she was a star for doing it. But as Pippa moved around the room she saw a few heads turn hastily away, and a few conversations broke off when she approached. She sat beside Lila. The strain of keeping a smile on her face made her cheeks ache.

'Going well, isn't it?' observed Lila.

'Yeah.' Pippa watched Freddie walk along a floorboard, arms outstretched like a high-wire act. 'Have the —' She broke off hurriedly. She had been going to ask if the police had been in touch, but if she asked then Lila might ask her, and she would need to lie. 'Have you started thinking about Christmas yet?'

Lila snorted. 'Started buying stuff in the January sales. And Bella's been at the Christmas catalogues already.'

Pippa sympathised, trying not to scan the room too obviously. God, it was miserable, this feeling of being constantly on the alert, of being spied on and whispered about. The sooner this was over, the better.

If it was ever over. What if they never found the murderer? And from what PC Horsley had admitted the other day, it was possible.

'I should go to the library,' she thought, and realised she'd said it aloud.

'Good idea,' said Lila. 'The one in Gadcester has book sales, they're great for stocking fillers.'

'Yes,' said Pippa absently, and checked her watch. Five to eleven. 'I should go and cut the cake,' she said

136

stretching. 'Nearly time for snack break.'

'I'll give you a hand.' Lila began to move, but Pippa put a hand on her arm. 'Would you mind watching Freddie for me, instead? Some quiet time would be nice. I'll call you if I can't manage.'

Lila raised her eyebrows. 'All right. Whatever.'

Pippa sensed eyes on her back as she walked to the door. *Stop being ridiculous*, she thought, as she pushed it open.

Some idiot had closed the kitchen door. Now she had to open it again. But it would be fine. Nothing there. She knew that.

But her hand trembled again as she touched the door. 'Stop it!' she muttered. She opened the door slowly, and peeped round.

The floor was bare. No body. No crime scene.

Pippa sighed with relief, found the wedge, and propped the door open again. 'There,' she said, brushing her hands together. 'Better wash them before serving.' She turned to the sink, and stopped dead.

On the fridge, next to the sink, magnetic letters spelt a message:

watch out nosy p parker

Pippa's knees gave way, and she grabbed the worktop to stop herself from falling. *Oh God oh God oh God oh God* . . . She gulped air but the room was starting to swim, and green and yellow dots twinkled in her eyes. She wrenched open the doors of the serving hatch. 'Lila!'

Lila's face changed instantly. 'Shit!' she shouted, and sprang up. Seconds later her arms were round Pippa.

'What is it? *Pippa!*' Lila gave her a slight shake. 'What's wrong?'

'Need to sit down,' murmured Pippa. 'Head between legs.'

'Yes.' Lila took her arms and supported her to the floor.

Pippa leaned against the cupboard, bent her head, and breathed slowly. In . . . and out . . . in . . . and out . . . The dots glided to the edge of her vision. When she raised her head Lila was staring at her. 'Sorry, Lila,' she whispered. 'Had a scare.'

'I thought you were — I don't know what I thought.' Lila was still holding her. 'What do you mean, a scare?'

'Look on the fridge,' said Pippa.

Lila's amused frown changed to incredulity as she read the brightly-coloured message. 'What the —!'

'I assume it's meant for me,' said Pippa. 'I think it's a warning.'

'The cheeky swine!' cried Lila. She started towards the fridge, then whipped round. 'You haven't touched it, have you?'

'God, no. I just nearly collapsed.'

'I hope this is someone's idea of a stupid joke,' said Lila grimly. She aimed her phone at the fridge, and took a picture. 'Evidence. You should take one too.'

'Yes. Yes, I should.' But when Pippa got to her feet and tried, the phone wobbled in her hands.

Lila took the phone and snapped a couple of pictures. 'What do you want to do?'

Pippa leaned on the worktop and thought. 'I should probably shut the playgroup and phone the police,' she said, slowly. 'But I don't want to let them win.'

'So what *do* you want to do? I'll support you — oh

heck.' Lila bit her lip.

'What's up?'

'It's eleven. I should be on my way to drop Bella off.' Lila ran her hand through her curls. 'It's OK. I'll text work and say Bella's ill —'

'No, don't. I'll be fine. Really. It was just the surprise.'

'I don't like leaving you. I hope it's a joke, but that message reads like a threat.' Lila opened the serving hatch. 'Nick, can you give us a hand?'

A minute later Nick stood in the doorway. His smile faded as he saw their faces.

'Nick, Pippa's had a bit of a fright,' said Lila. 'Someone's been playing the fool.' Nick's eyes followed hers to the letters on the fridge.

'Just help me serve at snack break,' said Pippa. 'I'm not closing.'

'What the —' Nick walked to the fridge. 'Have you touched it?'

'No!' Lila and Pippa said, defensively.

'Good.' Nick's expression hardened as he stared at the letters.

Lila put a hand on his arm. 'She needs looking after, and I need to go now if I'm going to get to work anything like on time.'

'I don't need looking after,' said Pippa plaintively. 'It was that first shock.'

'Yes you do,' said Nick. 'Go on, Lila, I'll handle this.'

Lila threw a grateful look at him, then hollered 'Bella! Coat on!' banged the serving hatch doors shut, and vanished.

'It's the same thing again, isn't it?' murmured Pippa. 'It could only have been one of the people who are in the hall now.'

'Try not to think about it.' Nick put careful arms round Pippa and she let her head sink onto his chest. She expected her pounding heart to be soothed, but Nick's heart was beating as quickly as her own. She could feel it through his shirt. Pippa raised her head inquiringly. His dark brown eyes were narrow with anger.

'It's all a bloody mess,' said Nick. He was looking not at Pippa, but over her head.

'I thought I was doing a good thing,' muttered Pippa.

'You are,' said Nick. He stroked Pippa's hair. 'But I'm worried. Someone reckons you're poking your nose in, clearly.'

Pippa gasped. 'Someone saw me coming out of the police station the other day. Maybe she thought —'

'What were you doing at the police station?' Nick's hand stopped stroking.

'I was getting the key for here,' Pippa said, as innocently as she could.

'Oh.' The stroking resumed. 'You should stay clear of the police station, then. It's probably nothing.' Stroke, stroke. 'Probably someone's idea of a joke.'

'Probably.'

'Just — be careful, Pippa.'

A cough from the doorway made them both jump, and spring away from each other. 'Need a hand with the tea?' said Sam, grinning broadly. The toddler holding her hand stared at Pippa with her fingers in her mouth.

'We're fine, thanks,' said Nick. He strode to the serving hatch and threw it open. 'Pippa, you cut the cake, and I'll get the milk —' He looked at his hand, gripping the handle of the fridge door. 'Oh, damn.'

140

'Well, if you're sure you're all right I'll get on with changing this nappy then,' Sam said to no-one in particular, and towed her daughter away.

'Oh God,' said Pippa. 'I should have explained about the message on the fridge.'

Nick frowned. 'I thought you wanted to carry on as normal. Once they know you've been threatened, and you're spooked by it, that'll be it.' He banged saucers on the worktop and brought a column of cups.

Pippa's mind raced at the speed of her heart as she unboxed the cake, got a knife from the drawer, and slid slices onto plates. Nick was right. But what Sam had seen would probably go round the playgroup like wildfire — and what if, somehow, Simon heard? *I'll have to tell him*, she thought, her insides screwing up at the thought of the conversation. *I bet he'll tell me off.* And she'd better tell PC Horsley — oh God, he'd think she was some sort of mad attention seeker. Pippa had been looking forward to a slice of Nick's cake, but now, though it smelled delicious, she couldn't have eaten a crumb.

CHAPTER 22

'Bit childish,' said PC Horsley, eyeing the letters on the fridge and writing in his notebook. 'Too vague for you to worry about in my view.' He paused. 'Are you worried, Mrs Parker?'

'A bit,' Pippa admitted. She had held herself together until the end of playgroup, but when the last toy had been put in the cupboard, the last cup washed and put to drain, and the last helper (Nick) waved off, she had closed the door and wept.

'Mummy?' Freddie put his arms around her legs. 'Hurt, Mummy?'

Pippa sniffled and shook her head. 'Not hurt, just . . . sad.' She began to stroke his hair, then pulled her hand away at the thought of Nick and, primarily, of getting caught. 'I'll be all right in a minute.' But she wasn't sure she would be.

By some miracle her phone showed a signal. Pippa took a deep breath and rang the police station. PC Horsley answered. Pippa gave her name and a brief explanation. 'I'll be round shortly.' The phone went dead.

'I've taken down the details,' said PC Horsley. 'Can

you give me a list of everyone who was at the group today?' Pippa nodded. 'All right.' He snapped his notebook shut. 'I'll be honest with you, Mrs Parker. It looks as if someone's taken a dislike to you.'

'Someone saw me leaving the police station yesterday,' said Pippa. 'A woman with a pram. She shot off when I waved.'

'Not much to go on,' said PC Horsley. 'If I were you, Mrs Parker, I'd keep a low profile. Don't talk about the murder. Business as usual. And definitely stay away from the police station. It's not worth getting yourself in a tizzy over.'

'I'm not in a tizzy —'

'Especially in your condition.' PC Horsley took a picture of the magnetic letters with his own phone. 'Now we can dust these for fingerprints, but I suspect whoever left this for you had the sense to wear gloves, given recent happenings. Anyway.' He reached into his pocket and brought out a pair of disposable gloves and a bag. 'I'll take these with me. Not appropriate for the church hall, is it.' He prised the letters from the fridge, dropping them into the bag one by one. 'Who else knows?'

'Lila does,' Pippa muttered. 'I called her in. And Nick; Lila asked him to help. She had to leave for work.'

'Did she,' said PC Horsley, in a flat tone. He sealed the bag and put it in his pocket, then pulled off his gloves and threw them in the bin. 'I'll give them a call. Don't want them broadcasting it.'

'Oh,' said Pippa. 'But —'

'But what?' PC Horsley's pen hovered above the page.

'Well, Nick gave me a hug, because I was upset by it all, and someone caught us . . .'

The notebook snapped shut again. 'Tell anyone who asks that it was baby blues, Mrs Parker. Tell them your sponge cake burned. I'm sure you'll think of something. Now if you'll excuse me, I've got a murderer to catch.' He put the notebook away and strode to the door, past Freddie who was playing Snap on Pippa's phone, perched on a plastic chair.

Pippa walked over to Freddie. 'We have to go now, Freddie, the next people will be coming to use the hall soon.'

Freddie gave no sign that he had heard her at all, his fingers still prodding at the cards on the screen.

'Now, Freddie.'

Freddie scowled, gave the phone one last prod, and thumped it into her hand. Pippa glanced at the screen to check for messages or missed calls. Nothing. Good. She locked it and slipped it into her pocket. 'What would you like for lunch, Freddie?'

'Tearoom? Pub?'

'Not today, Freddie, we're having lunch at home.' The thought of sitting with Freddie in either place, demonstrably friendless, made Pippa quail. What if people from playgroup came in, and started whispering and staring?

'Home is booooring,' said Freddie.

'All right. Fine.' Pippa racked her brains for somewhere to go. Sitting at home didn't appeal much to her either. 'Let's get out of here, anyway.'

Pippa locked the door and took Freddie's hand.

'Are we going home?' said Freddie suspiciously.

'To drop things off, before we go to where we're going.' Pippa said, playing for time.

'Where? Where?'

'Wait and seeeee . . .' Pippa's mind whirred as they walked along River Lane. Fishing in the river? Absolutely not, after what Freddie had caught last time. She unlocked the door and snapped the light on, as the cottage was still dark even at midday. No doubt Sheila would call that cosy.

Sheila.

Sheila was Barbara's friend.

Sheila might know who Shelley was.

'Where *are* we going?' said Freddie, standing in the porch.

Pippa looked around desperately for inspiration. The armchair, the fireplace, the — ah!

'We're going to the library! If it's open,' she said hastily. She scooped up her books and dropped them into her bag. 'And maybe we can buy something nice to bring home for lunch. What would you like?'

'Beans on toast!' shouted Freddie.

Pippa's bag dug into her shoulder as she walked Freddie past the neatly-raked piles of leaves on the village green. Lights were on. She crossed her fingers in her pocket. Please be open. And please let Norm be on duty.

The door to the country store opened and Henry charged out, towing Imogen. He had a bag of duck food in his free hand.

'Hi, Imogen,' said Pippa.

'Hi Pippa,' said Imogen, as Henry pulled her over the road to the green, kicking at a pile of leaves on his way to the duck pond. Was she imagining things, or had Imogen's greeting lacked warmth? Pippa told herself she was probably reading too much into it, and pushed the door to the library.

It didn't move.

'Ohhhhhh,' whined Freddie.

Tears pricked at the back of Pippa's eyes, and she blinked angrily. Such a stupid thing, such a little thing to be upset about! What was wrong with her? 'Come on, Freddie,' she snapped, jerking his hand.

Freddie didn't move. 'Want to go in!'

'It isn't open!' Pippa replied, louder than she intended. 'Fine, we'll do something else.' She looked at the green and Imogen, standing by the duck pond, turned away. 'Come ON!' She set her teeth and pulled the wailing Freddie along the road.

'Hold your horses, young lady,' said a mild voice. Pippa whipped round, ready to give whoever it was a piece of her mind to the effect that they had *no idea* what it was like.

Norm held the door open. 'I had to close up while I went to the loo.'

'Oh.' Pippa exhaled slowly. She still felt like crying.

Freddie tugged her hand. 'Can we go in, Mummy?'

'Yes,' said Pippa, and let go. He ran into the library, and she waddled after him. Now that her anger had faded, she was exhausted.

By the time she reached Freddie, he was sunk in a beanbag in the children's corner, gazing at a picture book. 'Shall I read to you?'

'He seems happy enough.'

Pippa caught her breath and put a hand on the bookcase to steady herself. 'Did you have to do that?'

'Sorry,' said Norm. 'The stealth thing stays with you. Anyway,' He put a large hand on her shoulder. 'I was going to ask if you wanted a cup of tea. I hope you don't mind me saying, but you look like you need one.'

Pippa put her hands to her face to stop the sobs coming out, but she was gone. She hurried to the other end of the library and cried big, noisy tears, her shoulders shaking. When she gasped for breath, a handkerchief was pressed into her hand. Pippa mopped her wet face, tasting salty tears, and hands guided her to a chair. She felt ridiculous, embarrassed, stupid, and above all, scared.

'I can be a listening ear, if you like,' said Norm, sitting in the chair opposite.

Pippa looked up, doubtfully, and he nodded.

'I'm frightened,' she said. 'I'm angry. I'm upset. I don't know what's going on. Someone threatened me today, I don't know who. I found a piece of evidence, and I don't know what it means. And I feel trapped.' She sighed. 'Is that enough to be going on with?'

'That sounds like you need a cup of tea and a biscuit,' said Norm, rising.

'Oh, and I've read my library books.'

'Ah yes,' said Norm, turning the little stack sideways to read the spines. 'Well, I'll get the kettle on, and you can ask yourself the big question.'

Pippa frowned. 'What big question?'

Norm winked. 'You know. What would Agatha Christie do?'

147

CHAPTER 23

'The thing is,' said Norm, 'you have to remember that Miss Marple and Poirot, and Tommy and Tuppence, and Sherlock Holmes didn't have to worry about getting on with life at the same time.' He dunked a ginger biscuit in his mug. 'That's the trickiest bit.'

After swearing Norm to secrecy, and with frequent peeks round the corner to where Freddie was flicking his way through half a shelf of books, Pippa had told him everything. The phone in the river, the call to Shelley, the magnetic letters, being caught in the kitchen with Nick, her conversation with PC Horsley. The whole shebang. And when she had finished, she felt better.

'Now, so long as I'm not a retired copper turned bad, you've done the right thing.' Norm slurped his tea. 'And let's be honest, I wouldn't be wasting valuable plotting time running the community library if that were the case.' He grinned. 'Shelley I can help you with. Unless I'm mistaken, Shelley is Mrs Shelley Jackson, headmistress of the primary school. I believe Barbara was a shining light and a permanent fixture on the board of governors.'

'So it was probably school business?' asked Pippa.

'Well, I'd assume so,' said Norm. 'You could go and ask, but given what happened this morning, I can see why you wouldn't. Anyway, I'm sure PC Horsley and Inspector Fanshawe will have that covered. After all, they've got her phone.'

'Yes,' said Pippa. 'I might still ask my mother-in-law if she knows her. I could pretend it's about getting Freddie into the local primary school. Well, I mean, I would want him to go to the local school. When it's time. That probably means I should already be sorting it . . .'

'Not right now,' said Norm. 'I think you should talk to your mother-in-law. Not just for information, but because she'll probably appreciate it.'

'I feel guilty now,' said Pippa.

Norm smiled. 'From what I understand, isn't that quite normal for mothers?'

'More guilty than that, even.'

'Exactly.'

'All right, I'll text her and suggest popping over.'

'Good. Sheila will probably give you chapter and verse on everyone in the village. And that would help a great deal.' Pippa looked up and Norm was studying her. 'For living here, in general.'

Pippa frowned. 'But I thought *you* knew everyone in the village.'

'To an extent,' said Norm. 'But as a police officer I met people either when they were having a crisis — which doesn't happen much round here, to be frank — or else at events. People tend to be very conscious of me, though I'm retired now. And most of your playgroup people I probably wouldn't know from Adam. I might recognise the faces, but that's it. Believe me, this murder is the biggest thing to happen for years. The papers are having a field day.'

'I've noticed,' said Pippa, making a mental note to find a wi-fi spot and read the headlines on her phone.

'And who else are you going to talk to?' Norm prompted.

'My husband.'

'And what are you going to tell him?' Norm grinned.

'Everything,' groaned Pippa.

'Not so bad, was it?' said Norm.

Pippa put her hands round her mug of tea and sipped. 'I know I should have, already,' she said. 'He's just so — busy with work, and never here. And I don't think he takes me seriously.' She sipped again. 'And yes, I should probably talk to him about that, too.'

*

Pippa left the library with a complete Sherlock Holmes (for variety) and a head full of Things To Do. Freddie shouted 'Leaves!' and shot across the empty road to the village green. 'Henry!' He ran towards his friend, who was throwing handfuls of leaves into the air. One golden leaf had settled on the top of his head, waggling when he moved.

Pippa followed, and after a 'We can't stay long, Freddie, we need to go home,' she watched from the bench. Hopefully Freddie would wear himself out enough to nap after lunch . . .

'Hi!' Imogen appeared next to her.

'Hi,' said Pippa, as neutrally as she could.

'Mind if I join you?' said Imogen, sitting down. 'Freddie seems better now. I'd have come over earlier, but he looked like he was being a handful. I remember when Henry got someone's attention he was always ten times

150

worse.'

Pippa smiled. How many times had she pretended not to see a child having a tantrum in the supermarket, to spare the stressed parent? 'He was, a bit. Luckily the library opened. Thank God for distractions.'

'Oh heck, yeah.' Imogen glanced at Pippa's stomach. 'I thought your bump was, um, a bit lower.'

'Yeah, baby's moving down.' Pippa rubbed the bump. 'It's a lot more comfortable.'

'Do you know what you're having?'

Pippa shook her head. 'We decided to keep it as a surprise this time. I guess we'll find out soon enough.'

Imogen laughed. 'I guess you will.' She glanced at her watch. 'Oh God, the time. Henry! Come along now!' She stood and waved her arms like an air traffic controller at the two circling boys, who both came running. 'See you Tuesday. Maybe.' Her gaze drifted down.

'It won't be this weekend, you know,' Pippa smiled. 'Nearly a month to go.'

'Hm,' said Imogen. 'I'm no expert, but I'd be surprised if you last that long.' They waved, and walked off across the green.

'Come on, tiger,' said Pippa. 'Time to fill you full of beans. Although you're full of beans already.'

'I'm not,' said Freddie, with a hurt look. 'I'm *starving*.'

'All right, all right!' Pippa levered herself off the park bench.

After lunch, despite protesting that he wasn't tired, not even a little bit, Freddie fell asleep five pages into the story Pippa was reading him. She crept into the bathroom, got relatively comfortable on the edge of the bath, psyched herself up, and rang Simon.

He answered on the seventh ring, 'Pippa!'

She had been expecting the phone to go to voicemail. 'Oh, hi.'

'Are you all right?'

'I'm fine. Well, not fine exactly, but yeah, I'm all right.'

There was a brief silence at Simon's end. 'It's not — you're not . . .'

'No Simon, I'm not about to go into labour.'

Another pause. 'I had to run out of a meeting.'

'Oh, sorry. I thought you might be on a break.'

'I did say I'd be in meetings all day today.' A short huff. 'Look, can I call you back?'

'Simon, I need to tell you — someone kind of threatened me at playgroup today.'

'*What?* What do you mean . . . who?' he snapped. 'What did they say?'

'Oh God . . . I don't know who. They left a message on the fridge.'

'What sort of message?'

'It just said *Watch out nosey p parker*. In magnetic letters. They probably didn't have enough Ps to do my full name.'

'So you've rung me to say someone put a silly message on the fridge at playgroup?'

'I was upset! There's been a murder, in case you've forgotten. I think I was being warned off.'

'Warned off what?' Another pause. 'Pippa, have you been sticking your nose in?'

'No!' Well, not exactly. 'I went to the police station to get the key for the church hall, and someone saw me leave. Maybe they thought I was . . .'

'All right.' Pippa imagined Simon shaking his head.

152

'Don't do anything silly, will you?'

'There's something else.' Pippa muttered. 'I had a bit of a wobble when I found the message, and a couple of people looked after me.'

'OK . . .'

'So one of them gave me a hug, one of the dads, and another parent saw. I couldn't explain myself because the police told me to keep quiet about the message on the fridge.'

The silence on the other end of the phone was thick enough to slice.

'I wanted you to know, in case anyone said anything,' Pippa faltered.

Still nothing.

'Simon, say something.'

'I give up. I bloody give up. I'll talk to you later. I'm too busy for this.' And the phone clicked.

Pippa stared at the phone, and then the tiles on the bathroom wall, for some time. She ambled downstairs and put the kettle on, looking outside and seeing nothing.

A knock on the window made her jump. Marge waved, and Pippa opened the window. 'Sorry, I was miles away.'

'You were,' said Marge. 'Away with the fairies?'

'Something like that,' said Pippa.

'Well, I won't keep you,' cackled Marge. 'Has young Freddie caught any more phones? And when's that husband of yours coming home again?'

'This weekend?' Pippa realised she didn't know.

'Tchah. Tell him I said hello.' Marge raised a hand and stumped away, followed by a clattering tartan shopping bag on wheels.

Pippa closed the window and switched the kettle on

153

again. She'd done one of her Things To Do, though it had been . . . disappointing? Not disappointing. Infuriating? No . . . She couldn't think what it was, exactly. But she felt like crying, again, and very alone.

CHAPTER 24

Pippa tried to balance a Garibaldi biscuit in her saucer while remaining reasonably upright in her overstuffed chair. It had been surprisingly easy to secure entry into Sheila's house. She had only had to phone and ask if Sheila would like anything from the bakery.

'Oh well, I really shouldn't, but it's important to support the local businesses, isn't it? I shop local whenever I can, so if you're going that way a Viennese whirl would be lovely. Yes. And perhaps a chocolate eclair . . .'

Pippa bought a box of assorted pastries, gritted her teeth, and drove to Sheila's house. She passed Laurel Villa on the way — beautiful, spacious, non-leaking, modernised Laurel Villa — and stared straight ahead.

Sheila's house was a square red-brick semi on a curving side street towards the edge of the village, with a Victorian-style street lamp by the door. Sheila took her time answering the door. 'Ah, Pippa, yes. And Freddie.' She looked at the box in Pippa's hand. Pippa held it firmly and smiled. 'Won't you come in?'

Pippa stepped carefully over the high door-sill and helped Freddie in, then followed Sheila to the kitchen. 'It's a bit of a trek to the village, and of course all those heavy bags . . . Tea?'

'Yes, please.'

Sheila took down a metal tea caddy and popped teabags into a round brown teapot. 'I should use tea leaves, but so messy . . . Barbara always said teabags were for lazy people. I had to hide them when she visited.' She smiled faintly. 'Poor Barbara.'

Pippa waited till they were settled in the lounge and Freddie was busy with her phone ('It isn't good for him, dear, all that flashing and beeping') before bringing up the topic of Barbara, and her friends.

'Oh yes, Barbara knew everyone, which is amazing considering she hadn't been here that long.'

'Mm.' Pippa sipped her tea and the biscuit slid in her saucer again. 'Were you her closest friend?'

'Well, I wouldn't like to say so, but yes, I probably was. She left me a little something, in her will.'

'Really?' Pippa shoved the biscuit with the bottom of her cup, and it plopped in her lap. She pretended not to notice.

'Yes. A pair of Royal Doulton shepherdesses which I'd admired. Very kind, but it has caused some bad feeling.'

'Oh?' Pippa managed to retrieve her biscuit, which broke in half part-way. She took a large bite of the remainder to dispose of it, then wished she hadn't since it was dry as a bone.

'Yes . . . I happened to mention Barbara's kindness at the WI meeting yesterday, and do you know, no-one else had been remembered at all. Shelley was livid. I mean, she tried to look as if she wasn't. But they were thick as thieves, with Barbara on the primary school board and all. I

156

believe she did leave money to the school — for a memorial piano — but nothing to Shelley personally.' Sheila preened a little. 'You've dropped a bit of your biscuit, dear.'

'So I have.' Pippa scooped the remainder into her saucer.

'I probably knew more about Barbara than anyone.' Sheila nodded, a faint smile on her face.

'I read your quote in the paper,' said Pippa. She glanced at Freddie, still absorbed in his blocks game. 'It was nice of you to contact them.'

'Well, I thought it would be nice for Barbara to have a testimonial. She was private in a lot of ways. Kept herself to herself.'

'It's odd that she moved here after her husband died,' said Pippa. 'I mean, most people — I would have thought —' she said hastily, 'would stay near their friends.'

'Ah, well,' Sheila's eyes gleamed. 'Barbara's husband didn't die.'

'Excuse me?' Pippa's cup rattled in its saucer. 'You mean . . . were they divorced?'

'Not even that,' crowed Sheila. 'Barbara was never married!'

Pippa's mouth dropped open. 'What?'

'She told me herself!' Sheila said, smugly. 'I was reminiscing about poor dear Frank one day, and Barbara said something like "Oh, well, I wouldn't know." I pressed her, and finally she admitted that she'd never been married. She told me that she made it up just before she moved to Much Gadding. I remember it clear as day. "It's hard enough getting old, Sheila, without being pitied as a lonely spinster. I get more respect as a widow than I ever did as a single woman. They think there's something wrong with you if you've never married." Oh, you'd have thought she'd swallowed a wasp. We never discussed it again, and of course I promised to say nothing. I considered phoning the paper when I saw her obituary, but in the end I decided a little white lie wasn't going to harm anyone.'

'No, I don't suppose it would,' said Pippa, automatically.

'Don't tell anyone, will you?' Sheila looked horrified. 'Barbara would kill me. If she could.'

'So Shelley didn't know?'

'I wouldn't have thought so.' Sheila frowned. 'You're very interested in Shelley.'

'Well, of course. She's the primary school head, and Freddie's coming up to three.'

'Mm.' Sheila didn't seem convinced. 'She's a nice woman, but easily led. Barbara used to say — in confidence, you understand — that she had Shelley eating out of her hand.'

Pippa sighed. 'It's a shame Barbara's . . . you could have put in a good word for Freddie at the school.'

'I probably could,' smirked Sheila. 'I don't know how the village will manage without Barbara. She kept things rolling along, you see.'

'Did I mention I've taken on the playgroup?' Pippa put the rest of her biscuit into her mouth. Sheila's expression soured a little.

'Yes, Simon mentioned it on the phone the other day. Is that wise?' Sheila eyed Pippa's bump. 'I mean, you are getting very big.'

Thanks a bunch. 'It isn't much work,' said Pippa defensively. 'And everyone's mucking in.'

158

'Oh good,' said Sheila, with an expression as if she had smelt a field of manure in the distance. 'Well, at least your little cottage must be easy to run. And that's a great help.'

'Good reminder, Sheila,' said Pippa. 'I must chase the estate agent this afternoon. I knew there was something else I had to do.'

Sheila looked dismayed. 'Oh, but isn't Simon handling it?'

'Simon?' Pippa laughed. 'He leaves that sort of thing to me. If it can't be automated, he doesn't want to know.' She shoved the memory of him phoning the water company to the back of her mind. The exception that proved the rule.

'Yes, well, anyway.' Sheila got up. 'I should be getting on with things. I've a cake to bake for bridge club tonight. Lovely to see you, dear. And Freddie.' She waved a hand at Freddie, still swiping at Pippa's phone.

'Freddie.' He didn't move. 'Freddie.' Pippa added a warning note and, eventually, Freddie raised his head, looking annoyed. Pippa was reminded of Simon's expression when she spoke to him in the middle of the football. 'We're going.'

Pippa chewed over her conversation with Sheila on the drive home, while Freddie babbled about how many blocks he had made disappear. What an odd thing to do, to pretend you'd been married. Although she could understand Barbara's reasoning, having met her. Pippa imagined Barbara fending off questions, perhaps advances, from some hopeful fellow-councillor, and deciding one day to invent a conveniently-dead former husband. What better way to silence people, and also get a bit of sympathy. Not that Barbara had seemed the sort of person who would care for sympathy. Pippa remember how she had shouted at

159

Imogen and Henry, that first day at playgroup, and shuddered. Barbara Hamilton had been a hard, merciless woman. And yet she had also done good things for the village. It didn't make sense.

Pippa mused. If this were a book, there would be some neat solution, like an identical twin. But would Barbara's identical twin be the good one, or the evil one? Snorting, she nearly jumped a set of traffic lights and came to with a start. She had driven most of the way home without paying attention. Pippa made a mental note to give herself a good telling-off later and focused on the road ahead until she was safely parked at River Lane.

Later, with Freddie asleep, Pippa allowed herself to play with the idea again. Might Barbara have been different before she came to Much Gadding? Could she have a murky past? Pippa gasped, and scribbled more frenziedly in her notebook. But how would she be able to find out? Barbara could have made a clean break from her past when she moved to Much Gadding. Pippa fetched the old newspaper and found Barbara's obituary. 'Mrs Hamilton grew up in Surrey'. But was that true? She couldn't even be sure that Hamilton was Barbara's real surname. More questions for Sheila. And what if Shelley knew something? From Sheila's account, she'd expected something from Barbara. In the meantime, surely there would be clues on the internet. Everyone was there somewhere; maybe in old newspapers online.

Pippa wrote *Research,* underlining it three times for emphasis, and her bump gave a lurch which made her feel sick. 'Don't you start,' she whispered. 'You've got ages yet.' She checked the date on her phone and her stomach lurched again. The midwife in London had said that second babies tended to be earlier than first ones. Freddie had been just over a week early. Her due date was less than four weeks away. 'Don't even think about it,' she hissed at her stomach. 'Not till we've escaped from this dump!' She rammed her notepad into the drawer, attempted calm, serene thoughts, and added *Buy decaf tea* to her mental shopping list.

CHAPTER 25

Pippa punched *End Call* and slammed the phone down on the table. First the estate agent, now Simon. What was going on?

Freddie looked up from his train set. 'Is Daddy coming?'

'I assume so.' Pippa huffed, and texted *Are you coming home this weekend or what?* She double-checked to make sure she was sending it to Simon, and pressed *Send*. 'Let's go for a walk, Freddie. There's no point wasting the whole of Saturday because Daddy won't talk to us.'

Or the estate agent. She had phoned them at 9.30, the minute they opened, to discuss the progression of the everlasting chain. Lorna or Donna or whoever it was had chirped brightly, 'One moment please, I'll get the paperwork.'

'Lorna?' said someone in the background (or Nora, or whatever).

'I'll just put you on hold,' chirped Lorna, and Pippa gritted her teeth at the muzak.

'Hello? Mrs Parker?'

'Yes?'

'I'm afraid I'll have to call you back. When would be convenient?'

'How about two minutes?'

'I'll see what I can do. Goodbye, Mrs Parker.' And Lorna rang off.

She didn't call back. And when Pippa phoned, at half-hourly intervals, the phone went to a messaging service.

It wouldn't have been so bad if she had reached Simon. But first his phone was engaged, then it went straight to voicemail. *Don't say you're working today,* thought Pippa. What was the point of having a family if you were never there? She rang a few more times during the morning, but after the fifth 'You are through to the phone of Simon Parker' she gave up.

'Coat on, Freddie, it's chilly.' Pippa put on her own coat and pulled her woolly hat from the pocket. Eventually, well wrapped, they bundled themselves out of the house.

'Tearoom, Mummy?' Freddie put his mittened hand in hers.

'You know what? Yes, we can. We deserve a treat.' She swung Freddie's arm as they walked along. The sky was blue, the grass still frosty and their breath puffed like dragon smoke. 'Do you think the duck pond will freeze, Freddie?'

'Let's see!' Freddie tugged on Pippa's hand, and she giggled as they hurried along River Lane, slipping a little on the glazed cobbles.

The ducks were still swimming happily in their pond, quacking at passers-by.

'They look hungry,' said Freddie. 'Can we get duck food?'

'Yes,' said Pippa. 'No sweets though, lunch at the

163

tearoom is your treat for the day.'

'And Daddy home.'

'Yes, of course.' Pippa said. 'And Daddy home.'

The same man was serving in the country store, but his oddity was diluted by a long queue; a three-way tie between newspapers, sweets, and duck food, with an occasional fat ball for good measure. Pippa made sure she had the right money for the duck food so they could escape with the minimum of conversation.

Pippa sat on a bench while Freddie sprinkled a trail of duck food. He was soon followed by a trickle of waddling ducks, which became a fast-flowing stream. He shook the rest of the bag onto the grass and toddled away, but a group of enterprising birds were still tailing him, quacking loudly. Freddie broke into a run, veering towards the pond. 'Mummy!'

Pippa started to get up. 'Freddie, come here!' But Freddie was too busy running from the ducks to listen.

'Shoo!' A tall figure ran towards Freddie, flapping his arms. Freddie stopped, gaping, and the ducks flapped too, rising into the air with outraged quacks.

'Thank you!' called Pippa to the man crouching with Freddie.

He turned, and it was Nick. 'Any time.' He took Freddie's hand, and led him to the bench. Grace trotted along behind them. Freddie's lip quivered a little, but he was doing his best not to cry. 'Nasty things, ducks. One bit me once on the finger. See, I've still got the scar.' He held out his index finger and Pippa inspected it solemnly. Sure enough, a band of paler skin showed above the second joint.

'What were you doing to the duck?'

164

'You don't want to know.' Nick grinned.

'No, I don't.' Pippa smiled back. 'We're going to the tearoom for lunch. D'you want to come?'

'Sorry, we've just been,' said Nick. 'I'd better get off home and tidy, we've got someone coming round.'

'Have fun.' Pippa wondered who it might be. One of Grace's friends, maybe, for a playdate . . .

'I doubt it,' said Nick. 'The estate agent's coming to take pictures.'

'Oh . . . I didn't realise you were moving.'

'Neither did I,' said Nick. 'I'd applied for the perfect job; more money, relocation package, near my parents so childcare on tap. So I assumed I'd never get it. I went for an interview three weeks ago, which I thought went just OK. They phoned me with an offer yesterday.'

'Wow.' The sun was so bright now that Pippa had to shade her eyes to see him. 'Congratulations,' she said, trying not to sound too flat. She stuck out her hand.

'Thanks.' Nick shook it. His hand was long, slender, and unusually warm on such a chilly day. 'A nice surprise at last.'

'Yes,' said Pippa. She felt she ought to say something else. 'We'll miss you. Not that we've known you long.'

'I'll miss you, too.' His hand still enclosed hers, and he pressed it lightly. Pippa remembered Nick's arms encircling her in the kitchen of the church hall, and her stomach did a little skip. 'I'd better go and sort the house out,' he said. But he didn't let go.

'Mummy, I'm cold,' said Freddie, jigging from one foot to the other. 'Need a wee-wee.'

Pippa sighed. 'All right, Freddie.' Nick released her hand. 'We'll see you around.' *But not for long.*

165

'Yes,' said Nick. 'Come on, Gracie.' He gave the hand that had been holding Pippa's to Grace, who grabbed it and skipped along by his side.

'Tearoooom!' yelled Freddie.

Freddie had his usual beans on toast (did baked beans protect against scurvy?), and Pippa treated herself to a cheese and ham croissant and a cappuccino. No more Nick. Despite the size of the croissant, she felt empty.

'Mummy?' She looked up, guiltily. 'Cake?'

'A small one.' She finished her cappuccino and watched Freddie demolish a jam and cream bun. Maybe the jam had some fruit in it. To be honest, today she didn't care.

'Are we going shopping?' Freddie mumbled, his mouth full of bun.

Pippa considered the contents of the fridge. 'We probably should.'

But she didn't want to.

Simon would probably think she was lazy.

Did she care? He hadn't bothered to text back.

'We'll go tomorrow. Daddy's car has a bigger boot.' There. Good use of logic to justify shopping avoidance.

'But Sunday is fun day,' Freddie whinged.

'Well, maybe Saturday's fun day this week.' Pippa spooned the froth from inside her cup. 'Shall we watch a movie in the armchair, with pillows and duvets?'

'Yeah!' Freddie bounced in his chair so hard that he nearly slid off. 'Can I choose?'

'If it hasn't got turtles in it, yes.'

Pippa left Freddie happily sorting through the DVD box (with instructions not to open any of the cases) while she fetched their bedclothes. She hugged the soft, warm mass to her, and buried her face in it for a few seconds. When

166

she breathed into the duvet, it made her face hot. She bundled it tighter.

Her phone buzzed halfway down the stairs. She carried on to the bottom, dropped the bedclothes on the carpet and worked her phone out of her jeans pocket. *Simon.* She'd have to keep it somewhere else soon . . .

It wasn't Simon.

Enter our prize draw NOW for a chance to —

She checked the ringer was on, and put the phone on the coffee table.

'PJs!' shouted Freddie.

'I don't see why not,' said Pippa.

'You too, Mummy! PJs!'

'Yes, I suppose I could.' A duvet day, that's what they'd joked about at work. Pippa shivered a little and turned the heating thermostat up. A duvet day sounded wonderful. The next time she got to spend a whole day in bed would be when she'd had the baby. If she got to do it then.

Pippa took Freddie upstairs and found fresh pyjamas for them both — Spiderman ones for Freddie, and a pair of fleecy flannelly ones for her. They were the only pair that still fitted; the elastic had gone around the waist so that Pippa had to tie herself in tightly to keep the trousers up. She put her towelling dressing gown over the top. *It's a good thing I'm just expecting Simon.* Her mind flashed back to the days when she would have arranged herself on their bed in something lacy and a pair of stockings. *Ha.*

She slipped *SuperMouse and the Cheese of Doom* into the DVD player, settled herself into the armchair, and Freddie, dragging the duvet along the carpet, climbed on top of her. It took a bit of wriggling to get comfortable, but

167

eventually they managed it, and Pippa tucked the duvet in at both sides. Freddie snuggled against her, and she pressed play.

After a few minutes Pippa's attention wandered from the cartoon superheroes flying in the sky — or was it space? Where had Simon got to? 'Freddie, could you pass me my phone?'

Where are you? She dismissed the idea of ringing. He was probably stuck on a station platform somewhere. And if he was stuck, he'd be grumpy. He'd probably be tired when he did arrive. Not much of a weekend, really. So much for the improved country lifestyle. Pippa looked at the screen. The superheroes were now fighting each other with lasers. She settled against the pillow. She might as well be comfortable if she had to endure this rubbish. How long were kids' films now, anyway?'

Pippa woke with a start as the door slammed. 'Woah!' Freddie snored on top of her. 'Simon?' She craned her head round, but couldn't see. 'Simon!' She shivered. It was Simon, wasn't it?

'Yeah, it's me.' Simon's voice was flat and angry. He walked into the room and stood on the borderline of Pippa's vision.

'Freddie's asleep,' Pippa whispered, pointing at the dead weight curled on her lap.

'I can see that.'

Pippa checked the time. Twenty past five. The DVD had finished and the menu screen was showing accompanied by a thumping soundtrack. 'Did you get held up? Why didn't you phone, or text?'

'I was busy.' Simon walked into the kitchen. The fridge door slammed. 'Jesus, Pippa, what am I supposed to eat?'

'You know what? Maybe if you'd bothered to tell me what your plans were I'd have gone shopping. Or maybe you could have come home this morning. Then I wouldn't be stuck doing the big shop by myself, would I?' Freddie stirred on her lap and she jerked her head angrily at him.

'I said I was busy.' Simon's voice rose. 'Fine. Here's my plan. I'm going out. You do what you like.' He picked up his keys and wallet from the table, and the door shut firmly behind him.

CHAPTER 26

Pippa dragged herself through the rest of the evening somehow. Freddie had slept for another half an hour, during which she had muted the TV and cried quietly. *That's it,* she thought. *I've had enough.* But what could she do? She was eight months pregnant, with a toddler, no house, and no job. Once Freddie was fed, entertained, washed, and in bed, there was no reason to stay up any longer.

It was past eleven when Simon came home. The key scrabbled in the lock, followed by the creak of floorboards, the scrape of knocked furniture and kicked boxes, and the muffled 'ow's and 'shit's of someone who has had a bit too much to drink and is trying to be quiet in an unfamiliar house.

The staircase creaked, and Pippa wondered what to do. Her inner voice shouted that Simon deserved a bloody good roasting for not phoning, for coming home late, and for storming off. But she was cried out, exhausted, and unwilling to start anything in the middle of the night. Especially because, given the thinness of the walls, the neighbours would probably hear every word.

'Pippa,' Simon whispered. 'Pippa?'

Simon's trousers dropped on the floor with a clink of the belt buckle, then other clothing flopped on top. The duvet lifted gently, just enough to let a draught in — thanks, Simon — and the mattress dipped as he got in, and again as his feet lifted from the floor. She could feel him looking at her, and tried not to screw up her eyes, even though the room was pitch black.

He turned over, tugging the duvet with him.

Pippa opened her eyes and listened to his breathing, punctuated by an occasional flump as he shifted in the bed. Gradually the movements grew less frequent. Her own eyes were closing, now he was home —

Well, sort of home . . .

It was light when she woke. She opened half an eye. Simon was next to her, wearing a T-shirt and reading something on his phone. 'Hello,' he said. 'There's a cup of tea next to you. It might be a bit cool.'

'Thanks.' She sat up. 'Where's Freddie?'

'Eating toast in front of the TV. I put cartoons on.'

'Oh. Right.' So cartoons with breakfast was all right now.

Simon put the phone on his lap. 'I'm sorry I walked out on you last night. I shouldn't have done that.'

'Mm.'

'We need to talk. I need to explain.'

'Yes, you do. Why didn't you call me, or text me, or anything?'

'I was angry.'

'I thought you were busy,' she snapped.

'That too.' He sighed, and smoothed the duvet around the phone. 'I had some paperwork to finish. Then Mum rang yesterday morning as I was heading off. She'd just come back from the village, and someone she knows had stopped her to ask how we were getting on.'

'What?'

'Yeah.' Simon's mouth twisted. 'Apparently this woman's daughter had seen you canoodling in the church hall. Or it might have been her daughter's friend. Mum wasn't particularly coherent.'

'Oh God. Sorry.'

'She was in bits. I was on the phone to her for ages calming her down.'

'I'm really sorry.'

'It didn't help that you'd been round the day before. When I told Mum you'd had a funny turn and the guy had been looking after you, she wasn't exactly inclined to believe me. She said you seemed fine to her.' Simon's eyes narrowed. 'And she also said you'd been asking lots of questions about Barbara. I thought we agreed you wouldn't poke your nose in.'

'We didn't agree. You told me.'

'Yes. I told you. And you didn't listen, and now you've had a warning. Which has led to my mum nearly having a heart attack.'

'All right,' murmured Pippa sulkily. 'I get it.'

Simon looked at the duvet. 'And there's something else.'

Pippa braced herself.

Simon picked a loose thread off the duvet. He drank some coffee. He smoothed the duvet again. 'I should tell you why I've been working away so much.'

There's someone else flashed into Pippa's head.

'I didn't mean to, but it's been building up over the last

172

few weeks.'

He's seeing someone at work. Pippa studied the pattern on the duvet, not trusting herself to speak. That's it, put our son in front of the electronic babysitter and break the news gently.

'All the evening meetings, the Saturdays . . .'

Pippa looked at Simon. His shoulders were bowed. His head was down. 'The firm's in trouble. Declan told me I should get out, he's getting out, but I want to stick by them . . .'

Pippa clutched his arm. She hadn't realised it was possible to be relieved and horrified at the same time.

'My job's at risk, Pippa. I got the letter from HR last thing on Friday. They're starting to lay people off.'

'Oh, no,' whispered Pippa.

'I didn't want to say anything unless I had to.'

A light switched on in Pippa's head. 'I rang the estate agent yesterday.'

It was Simon's turn to study the duvet. 'Yes.' He reached for his coffee again. 'They've been very good about it all. I'd asked them to deal with me, for the time being.' He drank, and cradled the cup in both hands. 'I've put Laurel Villa on hold, temporarily. We can't take a house on and lose it — we'd probably never get a mortgage again. And if I don't get something quickly, we won't be able to meet the mortgage payments. Not for long.'

A tear crept from Pippa's left eye. She blinked, and the warm wetness ran down her cheek. She tried to visualise Laurel Villa, but it was a blur. Probably it was just as well.

'So we're staying here?' Pippa imagined Sheila clapping her hands in joy that they were staying in

173

Rosebud Cottage — and Sheila's comment that she should leave the estate agents to Simon cracked her over the head. 'Wait a minute. Your mum knows, doesn't she? She knows about your job.'

'I —'

'You told your mum instead of me!'

'Yes I did. I didn't want to worry you, and I had to tell someone.' Simon's mug clacked on the bedside table. 'She's my mum, for God's sake. We talk a lot, and she knew something was up. So I asked her not to let on to you, and I told her. And it was a bloody relief.' Simon's mouth crinkled and Pippa saw he wasn't far from crying, either. 'Maybe I was wrong, but I didn't know what to do. I'm not even sure we can stay here, long-term. We've got some money from the flat, but this place isn't exactly cheap, and there's all the storage . . .'

'Oh God. Oh God.' Pippa imagined them living in one room, huddled in the middle of a pile of furniture which they were slowly burning for warmth.

Simon found her hand and squeezed it. 'It'll probably be fine in the end. But everything's a bit rocky at the moment. And being so far away, and worrying that you hated this house, and Much Gadding, and you weren't looking after yourself . . .'

Pippa returned the squeeze. 'I wish you'd told me before.' She steeled herself. 'Where did you go last night? Your mum's?'

His mouth twisted again, but this time with amusement. 'God, no. Mum isn't exactly my idea of a Saturday night out. I went down the pub.'

'The Fiddler and Flagon?' Pippa shuddered as she remembered the barmaid, the grinning, texting barmaid.

174

Simon saw her look, and put an arm round her. 'I behaved myself. But I did see someone from my past. The last person I'd have expected.'

'Who?'

'Oh, an old schoolfriend. Primary school, it's that long ago. We were best mates, till he moved away.'

'Wow,' Pippa said.

'I know! And the really weird thing was that Dom doesn't live here. He'd popped over for a drink. I mean, what are the odds?'

'Amazing,' agreed Pippa. 'So did you catch up?'

'A bit, yeah. We were reminiscing, mostly. And drinking. We've swapped numbers, anyway.'

'That's nice.' Pippa imagined a tall, broad man in a rugby shirt coming for Sunday lunch. 'Is he married, or anything?'

'Didn't get round to all that.' Simon grinned. 'He was a bit surprised I'd tied the knot. Wanted to hear all about you.'

'Ah.' Pippa imagined having her knee felt by this Dom under the dining table, once he'd had a couple of glasses of wine. If he drank wine. 'So, what are we going to do?'

Simon drained his coffee. 'We're in limbo at the moment. And I've been working such long hours I've barely had time to think. Declan's still with us in body, but his mind's on his new job.'

'What, he's already got something?'

'Yeah, he's off to some consultancy or other. Not one of our competitors — there's a clause in all our contracts. That's the problem.' Simon's face clouded. 'I'd have to step outside my comfort zone if I left. I've been with Azimuth a good few years now. I feel rooted. Good thing,

175

'cos now I've got most of Declan's job to do as well as my own.'

'That's pretty rubbish,' Pippa fumed.

'Yeah. But it happens, and you muck in.' Simon rubbed her arm, a little too briskly to be comforting. 'Anyway, at least nothing's public yet.'

'Can anything be done?'

'We're trying. The bosses are seeking deals with other firms. We might get taken over.' Simon sighed. 'No guarantee our jobs are safe.'

'Is there *anything* we can do?'

'Yeah.' Simon put an arm round her. 'Do a big food shop and deal with all my dirty washing.'

'Not exactly what I had in mind.'

'I know. But I've got to be in first thing tomorrow. Gerald — one of the directors — is reading my report this weekend and I'm in his diary for eight.'

'So you're actually at HQ?'

'For once. Although I'm in Northampton that afternoon.'

'Well, if you're not busy right now . . .' Pippa slid a hand under his T-shirt.

'Mummy! Daddy! Cartoons gone! M a n *cooking*!' Freddie wailed from downstairs.

Simon grinned. 'Knew it wouldn't last. All right, Freddie, I'm coming.' But he kissed Pippa before getting out of bed. 'Thanks for the offer,' he whispered. 'Maybe I'll have a window in my diary later.'

Pippa punched him gently on the shoulder. 'Imagine what it'll be like with two,' she whispered back.

Simon smiled. 'It'll be fine.'

CHAPTER 27

'Simon, where are we going to put those?'

'They're on offer!' Simon put eight tins of tomatoes into the trolley. 'They'll keep for ever.'

'Yes, they will. And we'll be tripping over them for ever.' But Pippa smiled. It was good to have him home, even if he was behaving like a big kid. And Freddie, sitting in the trolley, loved it. Simon dashed off again with the list he had so painstakingly made, checking all the cupboards. Half of the stuff he'd brought wasn't on the list. *So long as we have things we can all eat, it's fine,* Pippa whispered to her inner shopper.

What about the reduced to clear shelves, her inner shopper whispered back.

True, thought Pippa. She wheeled Freddie along to the bottom of the aisle. Several other shoppers had clustered and more were gliding over, like iron filings towards a magnet. A red-coated figure emerged from the throng, arms full of packets, like a rugby player exiting the scrum.

'Hello, Sheila,' Pippa called, leaning on the trolley.

'Hello, Ganma!' shouted Freddie, waving with both arms.

Sheila's eyes darted from side to side. 'Yes. Hello, Pippa.' She sidestepped quickly to a trolley parked next to the fish counter, and unloaded her bargains efficiently. Pate, ham, fancy biscuits, a small white sliced loaf, a couple of apple turnovers, a lasagne for one, two lamb chops . . .

'That's a good haul.' Pippa tried not to smile.

'One does have to live on one's pension,' Sheila said, a little stiffly.

'Yes, of course.' Pippa paused. 'And it is a local supermarket.'

'Hello, Mum!' Simon called, behind a wobbling box of nappies, with a mega-pack of toilet rolls balanced on top.

'Hello, dear.' Sheila waited until Simon had deposited his items in the trolley before extending her cheek for a kiss. 'Nice to see you two together for a change,' she added, a little barb in her voice.

'It's nice to be together,' said Pippa, smiling at Simon, who winked.

'Speaking of which . . .' he grinned at Sheila, 'any chance you could babysit Freddie for us, Mum? It isn't long till number two arrives, and a night out would be great.'

Sheila visibly withdrew. 'Oh well, you know I'd love to, but my diary is rather full, with bridge club and the WI, and er, my other commitments, and of course Christmas is coming —'

'Yes, of course,' Simon agreed. 'But I distinctly remember you were at home on Tuesday when I rang. So I assume Tuesdays are good?'

'Oh, er,' Sheila backed towards her trolley. 'I thought you meant towards the end of the week. Yes, perhaps a

178

Tuesday. If you're sure Pippa is up to it. She is getting *very* big now —'

Simon's brows knitted. 'Well in that case we'd better hurry. This Tuesday? After all, we don't want Pippa to give birth in the restaurant. Which she might if we leave it later —'

'Oh no — er, yes . . . Yes, Tuesday.'

'Great! Come for half seven. Freddie should be asleep, so all you'll have to do is watch TV. We won't be late home.' Simon grinned.

'I shall look forward to it.' Sheila approached Freddie and ruffled his hair, cautiously. Freddie giggled. 'Well, I must be getting on. Bye for now.' Her scarlet back tripped away.

'Nice work,' grinned Pippa.

'Still got it,' Simon slung an arm round Pippa and pulled her gently to him. 'I suppose we'd better get on with the shopping now.'

As predicted, when they got home (after a stop in the cafe for drinks and an iced biscuit for Freddie), the shopping filled the kitchen. The freezer was crammed, the fridge groaned, and tins were stacked on the worktop. 'Well, at least I don't have to worry you'll run out of food,' said Simon, finishing a pyramid of baked beans.

'I'll be in trouble if it falls on top of me,' said Pippa. 'I'd be buried for days.'

'Nah.' Simon turned the top can so that the logo faced forwards. 'You'd eat your way to freedom.'

'Thanks.'

After a lunch of beans on toast (which delighted Freddie immensely, although Simon complained that they'd ruined his pyramid), they put on a film to drown out the churning of the washing machine. 'God, it's noisy, isn't it?' said Simon.

'Yup,' said Pippa. 'You'll get used to it.' *And I could get used to it, with you here. If you'd only stay.* She was comfortable in the armchair, Freddie nestled against her. He had started the film on the edge of another chair, bolt upright, but after a few minutes he had climbed onto her. She had a distinct suspicion that his eyes were closing; his breathing already had the slow, regular rhythm of sleep.

'We need our sofa back, so you can put your feet on me.' Simon flung himself into the other chair. It's weird, you being all the way over there. I feel as if I need a megaphone.'

'The room's hardly big enough for that.'

Simon's phone pinged. He reached for it and opened the message. He whistled.

'What's up?'

'It's from Gerald.' Simon's eyes strayed to the phone again. 'He's sending Declan to Northampton on Monday instead of me.'

Pippa's stomach fluttered. 'Is that bad or good?'

'I hope good. He wants to workshop my report with the directors.'

How did you workshop a report?

'He wants me to facilitate it.' Simon sprang up and began to pace. 'Oh God.'

'But haven't you been trying to get yourself in with the senior team for years?' asked Pippa.

'Well, yes, but not when we're in the middle of a massive crisis. I don't want to be the scapegoat if it all goes wrong.' Simon paused in his pacing. 'Can I get my suit in at the dry-cleaners?'

180

'It's already gone three o'clock, Simon, you'll never get it back in time.'

'I s'pose.' Simon fetched his laptop and sat at the dining table. Then he returned and kissed Pippa on the forehead. 'Sorry, Pip, but I've got to make sure I'm ready for tomorrow. I'll make it up to you on Tuesday, honest I will.'

'S'OK,' said Pippa. 'I understand.' She gazed at the screen over Freddie's head.

Simon's phone pinged again. 'I'm not sure I want to look,' he muttered. 'Oh. Damn.'

'What?' Pippa was desperate to see, but Freddie was too high up her chest.

'The number I've got for Dom is wrong. I've just had a text saying *Who's Dom?*'

'That's weird. Still, he's got your number, hasn't he?'

'Yeah. So that's all right. I thought I checked it with him, though.'

'Well, he'll text you, anyway. Or maybe you can find his landline. What's his surname?'

'Percival,' said Simon, absently. 'I'm not sure where he lives.'

'Is it in one of the villages round about?'

'No . . . he said he lived the other side of Gadcester.' Simon tapped his pen on his teeth. 'Anyway. Better get on with this.' The tapping and slight occasional scratch of scribbling resumed.

Pippa shifted carefully in her chair under Freddie's dead weight, and wrinkled her nose as Freddie farted in his sleep. Despite everything, a good day. Simon was here, and maybe his report would somehow save the company and it would all be all right.

181

'Brew?' asked Simon. 'I'm going to make a pot of coffee. It'll be a late one.'

'A cup of tea would be great, thanks,' said Pippa. She'd lost the thread of the film completely. Someone was hurrying to get somewhere — or something . . . It didn't matter, she'd probably have to watch it another ten times with Freddie anyway. She sighed. At least she had a night off to look forward to.

'Here you go.' Simon put the mug into her hands and kissed her on the cheek. 'Erm, could you iron me a shirt or two later?'

'What's it worth?' Pippa whispered.

'An evening at Much Gadding's most prestigious nightspot.'

'You mean the Riverside Bistro, don't you?'

'Um, yes.'

'Oh go on then.'

CHAPTER 28

'Smash PR, you're through to Suzanna —'

'Hi Suze, can you talk?'

'You know I can.' A door shut. 'Not like you to call in the daytime.'

'No. But my head's wrecked.'

'Oh heck. What is it this time? Another murder? A bust-up with Simon? I wish I lived in a village, it's way more exciting than dull old London. Mind you, I am working on rather a fun account —'

'Suze, shut up a minute, will you?'

'I thought you wanted me to talk.'

'Yes, but not that much. I can't think. Freddie's been bellowing all morning.' They had met Caitlin and Eva in the tearoom, and played on the green afterwards. The noise throughout had been phenomenal.

'I'm all ears.'

'All right. Well, first of all Simon's firm are in bother and he's in a big meeting today with some sort of masterplan he's dreamt up.'

'Wow. Really?'

'Yes. That's not why I rang — although it's not

helping. And we might have to stay in this hole, or even move out, if he loses his job.'

'Oh God. Couldn't you move in with your parents or something?'

'You must be joking. Five — six — of us in a Highland croft? There would definitely be another murder if that happened. Anyway, that's not why I rang either.'

'Bloody hell, what else has happened?'

'Something small and stupid. But it's bothering me.'

'Go on.' Suze sounded as if she was doing the aural equivalent of staring at a TV screen.

'Well . . . this is probably daft.'

'No, go on.'

'Simon went drinking on Saturday night and ran into an old friend. Someone he hasn't seen since primary school. So they had a good old reminisce and swapped numbers.'

'I'm not gripped so far.'

'It's a slow burner, OK?' Pippa listened for signs of Freddie waking from his nap. 'So Simon sent this Dom guy a text afterwards, and it was the wrong number.'

'So he put the number in wrong. I assume he'd had a few.'

'Yes, but . . . anyway, I thought I'd find Dom's home phone number, as a nice surprise for Simon. So I looked in the Gadcestershire phone book, and there's no D. Percival.'

'Ooo. Weird. Maybe he's a ghoooost of Simon's old mate.'

'Very funny. He didn't say where he lived. And he asked loads about Simon.' *And me.* She stood up, suddenly uncomfortable.

'That's creepy. Wait — I've got it.'

'Really?'

'Yeah. This bloke wasn't Simon's school pal at all. Simon just thought he was, and rather than tell some tipsy stranger "You've made a mistake, I've got no idea who you are", he went along with it and gave him a fake number. He probably had a good old laugh afterwards. There you go, mystery solved. Can I have a gold star?'

'Simon seemed pretty sure it was him.' Pippa said doubtfully.

'Yeah, but it's been what, twenty years? And let's face it, loads of men look pretty similar. Anyway, got to go, I'm on a deadline. Ring me later?'

'Yeah, OK. Thanks, Suze.'

'Any time.'

But Pippa wasn't satisfied as she put the phone down. She fetched her notepad from the drawer.

Accidental wrong number?

Mistaken identity?

Ex-directory?

No landline?

Wanted to know about me —

Her mobile shrilled. *Simon.*

'How did it go?'

'Well, I've still got a job.' Simon panted as if he'd run for a bus.

'Are you OK?'

'Oh God yes. Fine. It went fine. Actually, no, it went better than fine. We workshopped the options and we're going to try for a merger. I've been seconded to the taskforce. Big meeting again tomorrow.'

'Congratulations.' Pippa tried to keep the grin out of her voice. Taskforce, indeed. 'So what does that mean?'

'Well, for one thing I'll be based at HQ, so I'll be home

185

every night. I can't swear to what time, mind. I predict a lot of microwave meals.'

'Don't be daft, I'll leave you something in the oven with a plate on top. Like a proper wife.'

'I'll believe it when I see it.' He already sounded much happier, as if a burden had been lifted. 'It's great to get stuck in. I felt like I was pinging round the country like a pinball while the ship sank in the middle.'

'Wow, that's a pretty mixed metaphor.'

'Whatever.' There was a smile in his voice. 'How are things at your end?'

'Fine. We've been with friends this morning and Freddie's wiped out.' She paused. 'Oh, and I've been trying to track your mate down.'

'Dom? What are you doing that for? He'll probably text in a few days. We said we'd meet up.'

'You're sure it was Dom? I mean, you didn't just pick on some random stranger?'

'Course!' Simon laughed. 'We talked about all sorts, our old primary school teachers and everything. God, Pippa, you're desperate for a mystery to solve, aren't you? At least it's not a murder this time.' He snorted. 'I'll talk to you later, OK? Got to grab something to eat before I go back in. Love you.'

'Love you,' Pippa said absently, as he rang off. She stared at the notepad. Maybe Simon was right. Maybe she was casting around for something to do. Simon had found his niche, which made him happy, and she was still looking for hers. *It'll pass when the baby's here,* she thought. *You'll have more than enough to do then, Pippa Parker —*

And something clicked into place in her brain. Pippa began to write, line after line, filling a page, filling another.

She broke off, panting, her heart thumping. She listened for Freddie, but he was quiet. If only she had a working internet connection!

Pippa flipped through her mental list of friends and acquaintances in the village, discounting most of them immediately. She couldn't trust them not to gossip — look at how quickly the news of her and Nick in the kitchen had got to Sheila. Norm was the obvious choice, if the library had the internet. But what if someone came in, saw her screen, and put two and two together? She'd already been warned once — and her mouth twisted at the memory, and what it had led to.

Who could she ask?

'Beyoncé!' came faintly from outside. 'Din-dins!'

Pippa got up and stuck her head out. 'Marge . . . I don't suppose you have a computer and internet?'

Marge left off banging Beyoncé's bowl with a spoon. 'Course I do. What do you take me for, some sort of antique? Beyoncé!' Beyoncé leapt from behind a bush and sauntered into Marge's cottage, tail bristling.

'Darn cat,' grumbled Marge. 'Is it for Freddie? I've got a few kiddie games but it's mostly shoot 'em ups. Oh, and Grand Theft Auto.' She smiled fondly.

'Er, it's for me, actually. I'm tracing someone we've lost touch with. As a surprise.'

'Like an ancestor? I've done my family tree back to the fifteenth century. Great fun. Full of cutpurses and vagabonds. That's the bonus of having an unusual surname, it makes us easy to find.'

'Yes . . .' mused Pippa.

'Where's the young'un?' asked Marge.

'Napping.'

'Ah,' Marge nodded wisely. 'Well, I'll get this cat fed and you can pop in when he's awake. I daresay I can keep him entertained.'

'Marge, you're a hero.'

'I know,' said Marge. 'Stop it, Beyoncé, you'll have me over.' Beyoncé was winding herself round Marge's legs, purring like a little engine. 'Cupboard love,' she snapped, and closed the door.

Pippa went upstairs. Freddie slumbered peacefully. Typical. 'Freddie . . .' She stroked his cheek.

Freddie flailed, and settled again.

'Come on, Freddie.' She tickled his neck, and he wriggled. 'Do you want to visit Auntie Marge?'

Freddie's eyes snapped open. 'To play?'

'Yes, to play.'

'Yeah!' He put his arms up to be lifted.

Pippa grimaced as she heaved Freddie out. 'Nappy change first! I think we should cut down on the baked beans, Freddie.'

Freddie pouted.

A few minutes later Freddie towed her along River Lane to Marge's cottage. 'Knock the knocker, Mummy!'

Pippa did as she was told and shortly they heard Marge grumbling to the door. 'Beyoncé! Shift!' She unlocked the door and peered round, and her expression lightened. 'Well, if it isn't my favourite fisherman!'

'Can we fish, Mummy?'

'Yes,' said Pippa. 'If Auntie Marge doesn't mind.'

'Course I don't mind,' said Marge. 'You'll need your wellies.'

Freddie towed Pippa to their house, urging her on like a racehorse. Two minutes later they were back, Freddie holding the wellies proudly, like a particularly special catch.

'Right, young man!' Marge rolled her sleeves up. 'You wait in the hall, I'll find the shrimping nets.' Pippa followed her in. 'I daresay you'll be able to work the computer better than me.' Marge led her through a cosy sitting room gleaming with brass, to a smaller dining room. A laptop stood open at one end. 'The internet password's Destroyer.'

Pippa smiled. 'Brilliant. Thanks, Marge.'

'Oh, and don't forget to clear your history afterwards.' Marge tapped her nose. 'If I don't know, I can't blab. Come along, Freddie!' She opened the cupboard under the stairs and retrieved two nets and a pair of green wellies. 'Let's see what we find this time!'

Pippa sat at the table and opened Marge's browser. It was odd using someone else's laptop — the icons and menus were all different. She searched, and scribbled in her notepad, and when the front door opened, with a resounding 'Cooee!', she couldn't believe they had been gone more than five minutes.

Beyoncé was sitting nearby watching her, very prim and proper. 'It's a good thing you can't talk,' Pippa muttered, reaching down to stroke her.

Beyoncé hissed and batted at Pippa's hand.

'Beyoncé! Naughty!' Marge strode in and the cat shot past her. 'Sorry, I should have warned you not to stroke her. She's a bit temperamental.' She frowned. 'She didn't scratch you, did she?'

'No, I was too quick,' said Pippa, showing her undamaged hand. Her brain went *ping*, and she wrote herself yet another note.

Freddie, who had been taking his wellies off, ran in. 'Mummy!' He threw his arms around her.

'Off!' Pippa disengaged him gently. 'Did you catch anything this time, Freddie?'

'Just stones.' Freddie's head drooped. 'No phones.'

'No, the phone was a one-off,' said Marge. 'And did you catch anything, dear?'

Pippa looked at the screen once more, then selected *Clear History* and closed the browser. 'Yes. I think I did.'

CHAPTER 29

'Can't you get someone else to do the playgroup?' Simon asked as Pippa straightened his tie. 'You shouldn't be hefting stuff around.'

Pippa pointed at Freddie. 'Nothing's heavier than him. Anyway, I have minions to do the lifting for me.'

'No change there, then.' He stooped and kissed her. 'I'll try to get home early. I haven't forgotten our hot date.'

'Glad to hear it,' Pippa called after him. 'Good luck!' He waved, and drove off.

Pippa went back into the house and put bread into the toaster. One thing about having Simon home was that they all got up earlier. She hadn't decided yet whether that was good or bad. It meant more time to get things done; after breakfast there would be plenty of time to clear away, put a load of washing on, get Freddie dressed, and do an errand or two before playgroup. It also meant more time to worry, though.

She arrived at the church hall at a quarter to ten. No-one was waiting. She unlocked the door. 'In we go, Freddie.'

'No one here.' Freddie's face fell.

'No, we're early.' Pippa opened the cupboard and lifted

191

a box of toys.

'You shouldn't be doing that,' Lila shouted from the doorway. 'A woman in your condition.'

'You sound like my mother-in-law.' Pippa tugged on an activity centre which had got stuck. 'Ooh!'

'What's up? Are you OK?'

'Yes, fine,' Pippa said, automatically. But she put a hand on her bump. She had felt a distinct twang.

'*Sit!*' Lila set a chair for her.

Pippa obeyed, but when the other parents arrived she pulled herself to her feet. 'See? I'm fine, now I'm moving.'

'How long do you have to go?' asked Catrin.

'Err . . . maybe three weeks? I've lost count.'

'What does the midwife say?' Lila demanded.

'Dunno, I haven't been yet. Next Monday.'

'You are kidding me!' Lila stood, hands on hips. 'I've a good mind to march you down and demand you get seen!'

'Please don't,' Pippa pleaded. 'I'm fine. It was just a twinge.'

'I've heard that before,' Lila said darkly. 'But I suppose you know your own body.'

'Yes,' said Pippa firmly, delving into her bag and waddling into the kitchen. She put the packet of ginger nuts on the worktop. Not that she needed the ginger for morning sickness — she was eating like a horse. But she felt queasy. She checked all the cupboards, just to be sure, and fled to the main hall.

'Hello,' said Nick. He stood in the doorway, holding Grace's hand. 'Sorry I'm a bit late.'

'You're not late, you're on time.' Pippa took him in. He had the slate-blue T-shirt on again. The one that showed off his lean torso every time he moved. That one.

192

'Yeah, but I meant to come early and help. Especially because it's my last time.' He wandered forward and women clustered round him, full of *Why?* and *What happened?*

Nick held a hand up. 'It's nothing bad. I got offered a new job, near my parents, so I'm moving. I managed to get a quick sale on the house, on condition that I'm out by the end of this week. So I'll be renting over there while I find somewhere permanent.'

'Wow,' breathed Lila. 'You don't drag your feet, do you?' Pippa wondered if she was the only person Nick had told.

'Well, congratulations,' she said, waddling over.

Nick's face clouded. 'Are you all right? You winced, I saw you.'

'Just indigestion,' said Pippa. 'I might go and get a ginger biscuit.'

'Yes, you do that,' said Nick, stepping back.

Getting to the kitchen seemed to take a long time. Pippa leaned on the worktop to catch her breath, holding the packet of biscuits. She would open them in a minute. When this cramp went off —

Nick came into the kitchen and started to fill the urn. 'You don't have to,' said Pippa.

'I want to.' Nick checked the lid on the urn and switched it on. 'You should be taking it easy, Pippa.'

'I know.' Pippa fumbled at the biscuits, but her hands were sweating and she couldn't get a grip on the packet.

'Pippa, shall I open those for you?' Nick held out a hand.

'Please.' He took the packet, pulled the end open, and handed it back. 'Thanks, Dom.'

Nick smiled . . . and the smile froze. Pippa put the biscuits on the worktop and moved towards the door.

'How did you —?' His voice was hoarse.

'Partly a hunch. Mostly trying to work out why Simon's old school friend would give him a fake number.'

'It seemed easier. I'm leaving, anyway. Not the time to dig up the past.' Nick walked towards her. 'I'd better see what Grace is doing.'

Pippa leaned on the door and looked at him. 'Once I'd discovered who you were, I wondered if you'd kept anything else hidden. Your wife isn't dead, is she?'

Nick bit his lip. 'No. Is there any point dragging all this up?' He moved towards the door again. 'Let me out, Pippa.'

'But someone did die. Once I knew your real name, finding your connection to Barbara was easy —' She gasped as a contraction twisted her stomach.

'I'm warning you —' Nick grabbed Pippa's wrist and pulled her away from the door.

'I found the newspaper report about your brother's suicide in prison. Barbara was the sentencing magistrate . . . Barbara Marshall, as she was then.'

'What do you want?' Nick hissed. 'What are you trying to do?' His grip hurt.

Pippa concentrated on keeping her voice steady and staying upright. 'Let go of me.'

Nick put his mouth to her ear. 'No.' His breath tickled her ear. 'I didn't plan it, if that's what you think. I came back here to start over. I walked into the playgroup, and there she was. But she didn't know me, why would she? It was so long ago. We both had different names. I thought I could put it behind me, but she wouldn't let me.'

'The day it happened, I came into the kitchen for a glass of water. She was talking to one of her cronies on the phone, discussing school places . . . I remember her face when she sentenced my brother. "We need to set an example", she said, the *bitch.*' His mouth twisted, and he blinked rapidly.

'She gave him the maximum. He'd just turned eighteen. A fight outside the pub. He was helping a mate . . . it got out of hand. Someone got a black eye, and he was the dope who got caught. First offence, but she threw the book at him. We appealed, but before it got to court . . . he was gone. He was gone.' Nick's voice cracked, and a tear ran down his cheek.

'"We must be careful who we let into the school," she said. The same smug, self-satisfied voice, after all that had happened. Stuart's death hadn't changed her one bit, but it devastated us. I saw red. The fire extinguisher was right there. She never heard a thing. I wiped it and put it back, I wiped the door handles, and that was the end of it. That *is* the end of it.' He brushed the tear away and took a deep, quivering breath. 'She's gone, and no one cares.'

'No,' said Pippa. 'I care. Innocent people are under suspicion because of you. Freddie found Barbara's phone, in the river by my house, where you chucked it after taking it from the body. I found you out, Nick. And despite your — attentions — I'm going to tell the police.' A sudden wave of pain shook her, and a sickening *whump* as the baby dropped in her stomach. 'Let go or I'll scream.'

'Go ahead,' said Nick, gesturing towards the noise coming from the main hall. 'I warned you not to stick your nose in, but you wouldn't listen, would you?' His voice sounded confident, relaxed even, but his face was tense,

195

and the hand gripping her trembled a little.

'Let me ring Simon,' Pippa gasped. 'The baby's coming. It's coming *now*!' She groaned as nausea washed over her.

'OK, here's the plan.' Nick's grip slackened a fraction. 'I'll drive you to hospital and drop you at the entrance. Then Grace and I will be gone. You keep your mouth shut, or I'll dump you in the middle of nowhere. That's the deal.'

'What about Freddie?' Pippa gritted her teeth as another contraction came.

'Someone will mind him. Now give me your phone.' Pippa dug into her pocket and handed Nick her phone, and a great sob came with it. 'Right, let's go. Not a word, remember.' He put an arm round Pippa, half-lifting her, and reached for the door handle with his spare hand —

The door flew open and a pack of police officers burst in. Pippa staggered backwards as Nick let go, and strong arms helped her to the side of the room. Nick was a blur of struggling slate blue, but two officers pinned his arms behind his back. 'Dominic Percival, alias Nicholas James, I am arresting you on suspicion of the murder of Barbara Hamilton.' PC Horsley snapped the cuffs on. 'You do not have to say anything,' he recited, 'but it may harm your defence if you do not mention when questioned something which you later rely on in court. Anything you do say may be given in evidence.'

Nick stood, panting, all his fight gone. 'Help me,' he muttered. 'I — Grace — she can't see this —'

Pippa bit her lip to focus on something besides what was happening in her stomach. 'Is your wife's number in your phone?'

196

Nick nodded, half-turned away. 'Ex-wife. Rhonda. She's twenty minutes from here.'

'All right. We'll call her.' Inspector Fanshawe put a hand on Nick's shoulder. 'Who can take your daughter in the meantime?'

'I'll text Lila to come in.' Pippa reached for her phone and remembered. 'Nick's got my phone. It's in his left trouser pocket.' PC Horsley obliged and handed the phone to her.

Thirty seconds later Lila burst in. 'Holy crap!' she cried.

Pippa gripped the worktop. 'I have to go to hospital!' She reached down her top and pulled off the wire. 'Ow!'

PC Horsley sprang forward and grabbed the little recorder dangling from the end. 'I'll take care of this, Mrs Parker. Worked a treat, you were clear as a bell.' Pippa was glad she couldn't see Nick's expression.

'Right.' Inspector Fanshawe drew himself up. 'Lila?' Lila's eyes widened even further. 'Can you take Grace home and look after her till her mum can collect her. We've got your details.' He turned to PC Horsley. 'Jim, take Mrs Parker to Gadcester District. Blues and twos.' PC Horsley nodded, casting an anxious look at Pippa. 'We'll move you when the coast is clear,' the Inspector said to Nick, who bowed his head and began to cry quietly. 'Bit of a mess, all round.'

'Come along, Mrs Parker,' said PC Horsley, giving Pippa his arm.

'It might need two of you,' said Pippa, her knees buckling. 'Freddie!' she cried.

'I'll take him too,' said Lila. '*Go*, Pippa.' She was smiling, but on the verge of tears.

PC Horsley jerked his head at a colleague, and between them they supported Pippa out of the kitchen.

'Is it far to the hospital?' gasped Pippa. She concentrated on the door approaching her.

'Not the way we drive,' said PC Horsley. 'But if you make a mess of my car I might have to arrest you.' He paused. 'That was a joke.'

CHAPTER 30

'This isn't the date night I had in mind,' said Simon, leaning on the arm of Pippa's chair.

'Me neither.' Pippa shifted about, trying to get comfortable. 'But at least we're home.' She looked at the tiny bundle in her arms. 'Trust baba to arrive early.'

'Yes.' Simon stroked the little bit of exposed red cheek. 'Wait till Freddie hears he's got a sister.'

'Do you think he'll mind?' Pippa reached for her mug of tea.

'Nah.' Simon kissed the fuzz of black hair, and then kissed Pippa. 'I'd better go and fetch him. Mum won't drive in the dark.' But he didn't move. 'How did you work it all out?'

'Well, I was trying to find Dom . . . I was talking to myself and the penny dropped as soon as I said *Pippa Parker.*'

'I don't get it,' Simon frowned.

'Well, I wasn't always Pippa Parker, was I? What I mean is, women change their name quite a lot, getting married, or divorced of course . . . Men don't. Dom clearly didn't want you to find him again, seeing as he gave you a fake number, and didn't say where he lived. But it's easy to find anyone on the web these days. Unless he was going under a different name. So I started thinking, and I got suspicious.'

'Was that why you sent me that odd text yesterday? About interesting scars?'

'Yes. Nick had a scar on his finger — he showed Freddie — and he said he'd been bitten by a duck as a kid. I figured it was worth a try. You were probably the only person here who'd remember. And who would recognise a kid who left the village twenty years ago as the same person, apart from his best friend?'

'He really was bitten by a duck. Stitches and everything. I'd forgotten until you texted.' Simon's smile vanished as quickly as it came. 'Poor bloke. Hopefully they'll reduce it to manslaughter.'

'He was all ready to leave. House sold and everything. But I thought he'd come to playgroup one last time, to say goodbye. Everyone loved him. I went to see PC Horsley, and we cooked up the idea of the wire.'

'So it was the detective skills of Pippa Parker that nabbed him.'

'It's weird,' mused Pippa. 'Two people who were making a fresh start, and they cross paths again.'

'Oh God. I remember Stuart. He was maybe four years older than us.'

'I know. Nick would have been, what, fourteen when it happened. So young.'

'I wish I'd known. I wish we hadn't lost touch.'

Pippa rubbed Simon's arm. For a moment she wondered what Nick would have been like if none of it had happened, if Barbara had let his brother off with a warning . . . She sighed. It was done now, and she — they — would never know.

Simon got up. 'I'm going to ask Marge to come over. I don't want to leave you on your own.'

'OK.' Pippa shifted cautiously among her cushions. 'Are you going to tell her the name?'

'You can. I'll tell Mum when I get there. Have you rung your parents?'

'Not yet. I've been busy.' Pippa smiled up at him. 'How did your — thing — go?'

'The meeting?' Simon paused, his hand on the door. 'It was — actually, it was good. Zenith are keen. In fact, we've even got a name.'

'Must be a day for it,' smiled Pippa. 'Go on, then.'

Simon sketched a banner with his hands. 'Fusion. Whaddya think?'

'Nice. Short and snappy. Easier to spell than Azimuth, too.'

'There is that.'

'Do you have a date?'

'Well, there's all the 'i's to dot and 't's to cross, but . . . maybe next month.'

'Before Christmas?'

'Before Christmas. Oh, and I have a new job title. Transition Team Head.'

'Cool. Does it come with more money?'

'I'm hoping so. And it's based at HQ.'

'Marvellous,' Pippa grinned. 'Congratulations. Does that mean we're back on with Laurel Villa?'

'It sure does.' Simon looked around. 'And the quicker the better.'

'I'll second that,' said Pippa, surveying the room, which

was piled with baby paraphernalia. 'It'll be worse when we get the stuff from storage. And speaking of getting things, go and get Freddie.'

'All right! All right!' Simon held his hands up and backed out of the door.

Pippa closed her eyes, sinking into the embrace of the chair. She jumped as her phone pinged. She reached carefully over the baby's head. *Are you OK? Lila* x. She smiled and texted *All good. At home. It's a girl! Knackered speak soon P x*. All in all, it *had* been a tiring day. Playgroup on its own was taxing, but coupled with detective work . . . *I wasn't scared, though*, she thought, rather proudly.

That's because you knew a load of policemen were listening in on your wire, her more logical self retorted.

I was still very brave . . . Pippa's lip quivered a little as she visualised herself confronting Nick, before she remembered that she had actually spent most of the exchange doubled up with pain.

Even through the horrible waves of nausea, Pippa had been secretly thrilled to be driven at top speed to the hospital. PC Horsley had looked across at her approximately every thirty seconds as they raced along, until Pippa had to ask him to watch the road. He screeched to a halt outside the hospital doors and he and his colleague practically carried her to the reception, where the desk clerk gave Pippa an old-fashioned look.

'She's about to give birth!' snapped PC Horsley. 'Crack on, will you?'

The desk clerk transferred her disdain to the policeman, turning to Pippa with a sympathetic air. 'Have you got your notes, dear?'

'I've got nothing.' Pippa clenched her teeth. 'I must text my husband — urrarrgh!' Her head disappeared beneath the counter as she fought another contraction.

'Never mind.' The clerk pushed a form on a clipboard across the counter. 'Hang on in there, dear. We'll get you sorted out in a tick.'

Pippa gripped the pen like a lifeboat and filled the form in between gasps. When she had finished a midwife was at her shoulder. 'We'd better get you in. Can you walk, or do you need a chair?'

'We can help,' said PC Horsley.

'I can walk,' said Pippa. She took a step away from the counter and her knees gave way as a wave of pain crashed into her. The policemen grabbed her again just in time.

'I'll get a chair.' The midwife dashed off, and presently Pippa zoomed along the corridor, clutching the arms of a rickety wheelchair. It felt as if they were going faster than the police car.

Five minutes and one very big push later, it was all over. The midwife wrapped up a squirming, bright red bundle and handed it to Pippa. 'She's lovely. Ten fingers, ten toes, six pounds thirteen ounces. Only the afterbirth now, and that can wait.' She paused. 'Should I tell one of the policemen?'

Pippa gasped. 'I haven't told Simon!' She tried to look for her bag, but she was scared of falling off the high, narrow bed. 'Could you pass me my bag, please? I must text him.'

The midwife took off her gloves and complied. 'Phone him,' she smiled. 'It is big news.'

Pippa rummaged for her phone. 'He's in a big meeting . . .'

'It can't be *that* big.' The midwife put her hand on Pippa's shoulder.

Pippa rang Simon's number, feeling faintly told-off. She was surprised when he answered. 'Pippa, hi . . .'

'It's a girl, Simon. I mean, she's a girl.' Pippa looked down at the gnarled little hands peeping out of the blanket.

'Oh my . . . no! What, already? Congratula — where are you?'

'Gadcester District.'

'Right, I'm on my way. Do I need to bring anything?'

'Erm . . . clean clothes? Changing bag — it's got newborn nappies in, I think . . . Oh, and Freddie's with Lila. I'll text you her number in a minute.'

'Right, I'm on it. I'll be there as soon as I can. Love you.' He rang off.

Pippa put the phone on the bed. 'Are you going?' she asked the midwife heading for the door.

The midwife paused, sheepishly. 'I was just going to tell the policemen everything's fine. One of them seemed rather worried.'

Pippa giggled. 'You didn't see him in the police car.'

Forty minutes later Simon walked in, changing bag slung over his shoulder. 'Sorry I haven't brought flowers,' he said, kissing her. 'I understand you had a police escort.' He raised his eyebrows at Pippa.

'It's been quite a morning. She's asleep, or I'd let you have a go.'

Simon peered into the folds of blanket. 'I'd forgotten how small they are.'

'I'll leave you two alone.' The midwife paused at the door. 'You should be able to go home this afternoon, now baby's had a feed.'

And now they were home, Rosebud Cottage seemed almost cosy. Simon had rung Sheila and asked her to fetch Freddie from Lila's. 'It'll do her good to get some practice in,' he said, smiling. 'Actually, she sounded pleased.' They had spent most of the rest of their time in hospital gazing at the baby and talking softly.

'Only me,' stage-whispered Marge, tiptoeing in. 'Is baby asleep?'

Pippa nodded. Marge closed the door, then crept across and peered. 'Can't see a darn thing.' She peered at Pippa. 'And how are you?'

Pippa smiled. 'I'm fine.' She really was. She felt better than she had since moving in.

'Your husband says you've been catching criminals.' Marge jerked a thumb outside.

Pippa grinned. 'Just the one.'

'Jolly good. Although I imagine you'll be busy with baby now. Does she have a name yet?'

'She does.' As if on cue, a wriggle and a little mew issued from the bundle in her arms. Pippa pulled the blanket down a little, and met round, dark blue eyes. 'May I introduce . . . Ruby Tuesday Parker.'

'Bless.' Marge put out a finger. 'My, she's got a grip! Maybe you'll be catching criminals too one day, young lady.' Ruby stared in her direction and burped.

'Let's wait and see,' said Pippa. 'It's a lot harder than you think.'

ACKNOWLEDGEMENTS

First of all, thank you to everyone who read and commented on the manuscript of *Murder At The Playgroup*: Ruth Cunliffe, Laura Dunaway, Paula Harmon, Judith Leask, Bobbi Lerman, Thérèse Markham, and Gaynor Seymour.

Thanks as always to John Croall for his meticulous proofreading. Any errors which remain are entirely down to me. At least this time I couldn't make any historical blunders!

And a big thank you to Bold Street Writers, who have endured various bits of *Murder* being produced in our writing sessions. 'This is part of something bigger' is fast becoming my catchphrase. So a message for Pat F, Pat H, Pat L, Margaret H, Margaret K, Margaret U, Shauna, Eileen and Gerry — I can't promise I'll stop (especially since I started the next book by accident last week), but thanks for putting up with me!

But as ever, the biggest thanks are to my husband Stephen Lenhardt. Beta-reader, cheerleader (not literally!), soother of writerly paranoia, and excellent cook, he is the best partner a writer could have.

Finally, thank you for reading *Murder At The Playgroup*. I hope you've enjoyed it, and if you would like to leave a short review on Amazon, Goodreads or elsewhere, I'd really appreciate it.

FONT AND IMAGE CREDITS

Fonts:

MURDER font: Edo Regular by Vic Fieger (freeware): www.fontsquirrel.com/fonts/Edo

Magnetic letters font: League Spartan by The League of Moveable Type: www.fontsquirrel.com/fonts/league-spartan. License — SIL Open Font License v.1.10: http://scripts.sil.org/OFL

Script font: Dancing Script OT by Impallari Type: www.fontsquirrel.com/fonts/dancing-script-ot. License as above)

Graphics:

Hall: Fort by nightwolfdezines: www.vecteezy.com/vector-art/90185-free-fort-in-flat-vector-design

Church: taken from Simple Country Church vectors by ayaankabir: www.vecteezy.com/vector-art/90090-simple-country-church-vectors

Houses: pink and yellow and blue by MiniStock: www.vecteezy.com/vector-art/116363-vector-house www.vecteezy.com/vector-art/109144-vector-townouses. Blue and white awning and red/green houses by happy me luv : www.vecteezy.com/vector-art/91211-colourful-houses-icons

Trees: taken from Free Tree vector by nightcharges (edited and recoloured): www.vecteezy.com/vector-art/101875-free-tree-vector

Benches: taken from park vector by nightcharges: www.vecteezy.com/vector-art/131274-free-park-vector

Ducks: taken from toy icons by jellyfishwater (edited and recoloured) : www.vecteezy.com/vector-art/140022-silhouette-toy-icon-vectors

Cat: freevector (recoloured): www.vecteezy.com/vector-art/78073-halloween-animals-silhouettes

Cover created using GIMP image editor: www.gimp.org.

ABOUT THE AUTHOR

Liz Hedgecock grew up in London, England, did an English degree, and then took forever to start writing. After several years working in the National Health Service, a corporate writing course rekindled the flame, and various short stories followed. Some even won prizes. The stories started to grow longer — and then the murders began . . .

Liz's reimaginings of Sherlock Holmes, and *Bitesize*, a collection of flash fiction, are available in ebook and paperback.

Liz now lives in Cheshire with her husband and two sons, and when she's not writing or child-wrangling you can usually find her reading, messing about on Twitter, or cooing over stuff in museums and art galleries.

Website/blog: http://lizhedgecock.wordpress.com
Facebook: http://www.facebook.com/lizhedgecockwrites
Twitter: http://twitter.com/lizhedgecock
Goodreads: https://www.goodreads.com/lizhedgecock

OTHER BOOKS BY LIZ HEDGECOCK

The Secret Notebook of Sherlock Holmes
A Jar Of Thursday
A House Of Mirrors
The Case of the Snow-White Lady
Bitesize

Pippa Parker will return in

MURDER
in the
Choir

Peril on the high Cs...

Printed in Great Britain
by Amazon

59179682R00128